Rhythm Can't Keep Time

Sometimes Love Just Ain't Enough

DEONDRIEA CANTRICE

Way, Inc
Prosper, Texas

This book is a work of fiction. The events and characters described herein are imaginary and are not intended to refer to specific places or living persons. The opinions expressed in this manuscript are solely the opinions of the author and do not represent the opinions or thoughts of the publisher.

Way, Inc

ISBN: 979-8-8689-6416-9

PRINTED IN THE UNITED STATES OF AMERICA

Dedication

In Loving Memory of
Calvin "Luke" Graham
Thank you for your words of
wisdom and encouragement

Acknowledgements

I appreciate the love, support, and encouragement of my friends Darlene Brandon and Leila Schaub. Your friendship has inspired me to use my God given talent to pursue my dreams. I value your feedback and patience; you hold a special place in my heart.

Special thanks to Pat Dodd, thank you for being my mentor and my friend. Christopher P. Johnson, this book would not have been possible without you.

Chapter I

I guess I am just a glutton for pain. I reluctantly agreed to entertain Sabrina for the weekend, only because I didn't know how to say HELL NAW, without it coming out the wrong way. Sabrina was a former co-worker that relocated from Denver to Atlanta, and she was back in Denver for a long weekend. I know next time not to say, *here's my number look me up the next time you are in Denver* unless I really mean it. She was one of those people that I could only take in small doses.

Sabrina was in town the weekend of the Summer Jazz Fest and she wanted you know who to take her. We were not friends like that, I thought. I only befriended her because there were only a few blacks at our organization. My intent from the beginning was to strictly be friends at the office. I never spent time with her outside of work, but for some reason, she was excited that we were gonna hang out. You would think I learned my lesson the first time I made a public appearance with her.

One afternoon, Sabrina, about 6 of our co-workers, and I decided to go to Greta's Supper Club for lunch. Greta's was a soul food restaurant and bar in the hood. The service at Greta's was crappy, but the food was worth the lack of professionalism and nasty attitudes. The entire group ordered Greta's specialty, the catfish sandwich. As we finished eating lunch, the waitress returned with our check. Without even looking at the bill, everyone threw a ten-dollar bill on the table not expecting change. In fact, the group's conversation didn't stop. I noticed Sabrina pulled a calculator out of her purse to figure out "her portion" then searched her wallet for exact change. The table became quiet when she looked up from her purse and asked, "Do you think we should leave a tip?" She then placed the exact change on the table. That was when I found out that Sabrina was a self-proclaimed class act, but in actuality, she was an embarrassing penny pincher. Sabrina didn't know restaurant etiquette, so why did I think it would be ok to take her somewhere for a weekend.

The Jazz Fest is held annually in Winter Park, a ski resort about 100 miles outside of Denver. The Jazz Fest consisted of 12 jazz artists that performed live on stage. By day, we sat on the side of the mountain enjoying live Jazz, visiting booths, and socializing. By night, it was just one huge party. Denver's finest adult crowd usually showed up for this event. The Jazz Fest was off the hook no matter what artists were performing. The finest brothas came out the woodwork. It was an ideal weekend. We partied hard, took in the scenery, and listened to jazz. A girl was destined to meet several potential boos even if she wasn't in the market. We don't have too many events like this in Colorado, so we make the best of the few that we do have.

There was an assortment of things that I would rather do with my weekend besides being with Sabrina because I couldn't have real fun with her as my sidekick. Sabrina was that friend we all have that sits back and passes judgment on what everybody around her is doing, never acknowledging the crypt that she called her personal life. She was quick to tell what you did, never confessing her own indiscretions. Damn, how did I wind up in this situation?

The Jazz Fest was a little pricey for most hood rats and too far of a drive for the rough necks. It was the prime place for the upscale, adult crowd. Most people rented a condominium or house for the weekend, heading up on Friday to party and prepare for the weekend. Saturday morning, at about 10am, the first artist mounted the stage and the concert lasted until about 6pm. The weekend was for whites, blacks, couples, singles, young and old. Hundreds of people camped out in front of the stage in lawn chairs or blankets, equipped with coolers and picnic baskets. There was something about the atmosphere that made the event pleasurable even if you weren't a jazz fan.

Every year, my mother and her friends rented a huge fully furnished house on top of this hill for the Jazz Fest. The house comfortably slept 16 people. Against my better judgment, I agreed to take Sabrina to the house because I was not trying to entertain her all weekend at a condo of our own.

Sabrina and I headed to Winter Park on Saturday after the concert with just enough time to chill before the parties began. I decided this would be best, that way I wouldn't have to spend too much quality time with her. The downside to this situation was a sista couldn't get her freak on and really kick it. Going up later, I could pawn her off on some unsuspecting sap and meet me a boo in the process. Don't get me wrong, she was cute. Sabrina had a perfect honey brown complexion, and had curves in all the right places, but she could wear out your reserved nerve.

After arriving in the resort town, we went directly to my mom's place to chill, eat, and get dressed for the evening. As usual, my mom's place was unquestionably the happening spot. There were cases of ribs, steaks, catfish, every side dish you could think of and a completely stocked bar. Tyson, a family friend was the resident chef and man he knew how to throw down. He was one of those corn fed, strapping lads that would make your mouth water over a sandwich. My thought was we might as well enjoy a damn good meal for free rather than mediocre take out for a price.

We ate, drank, and laughed until we got fat, full, and partly cloudy or shall I say slightly tipsy then headed to the nightclub. If I would have had one more sip or another fork of spaghetti, I would have been done for the night. Niggaitis was truly about to set in and the evening would have been a wrap.

Being irritated by Sabrina's general presence, I made sure I blended in with the crowd until it was time to go. We were in and out of my mom's place in record time, but I shot myself in the foot because that meant we arrived at the party early and I was forced to spend one on one time with her. I didn't understand it. Sabrina had a lot going for herself. She wasn't married, didn't have any kids, and she had a successful career. Why did she go out of her way to be so damn irritating?

Sabrina was a real-life gold digger. She would date anyone that she thought had money. She didn't discriminate against looks, age, race, or marital status. Everybody got their hustle, but the thing that confused me about Sabrina is she watched the "How To Be A Player" informational, but didn't attend the seminar. She slept with men on the first date, told them about all her other sexual escapades, then tried to pimp him for money. She never even took the time to find out if these men had money or more importantly, did they share? I might be wrong, but shouldn't you ask for what you want before dropping your drawls?

Chapter II

You could hear the bass of the music thumping outside the club. I was partly cloudy and ready to party. Sabrina and I went inside the club to find the DJ and about 10 people holding up the walls. I hoped this was not an indication of what the evening had in store because I was trying to get into some situations and circumstances. It was summer and I was looking for a whole for real cute boo. Sabrina was on the prowl for a sugar daddy or someone that would take care of her. We agreed to leave the club and come back when it was popping. After getting our hands stamped so that we could re-enter the club, Sabrina and I sat in the car and listened to music with hopes that the crowd would soon fill in.

While sitting outside the club waiting for the crowd to arrive, a shiny, black convertible Mercedes pulled up beside the passenger door. I was intrigued for a hot second until I recognized the driver as Maxwell Walker, a professional football player for Denver.

"Are ya'll about to leave?" Sabrina just sat cheesing like a Cheshire cat. I leaned forward and asked,

"Why? Are you looking for a parking space?" Maxwell nodded.

Trying to help a brotha out I replied, "No we are not leaving, but I will back up a tad and you can park adjacent to us if you want."

"That'll work, good looking out." Maxwell responded.

"Girl, the passenger is fine, do you know them?" Sabrina was definitely money hungry because neither one of them qualified as fine, in fact, I couldn't rate them as cute.

"I don't know them, but the driver plays football for Denver." Why did I say that to Sabrina? She immediately perked up, stuck out her chest, and refocused her attention on Maxwell. That was too funny because Maxwell was a little hard on the eyes. I didn't recognize the passenger, and Sabrina never even waited to see if he played ball also. Low and behold, we later found out that the passenger was Grant Stephenson and he played for Arizona. After parking, Maxwell and his friend approached my car door.

"Is it poppin' inside?"

"Naw, ain't nobody in there yet. The parking up here is scarce and I'm not trying to lose my spot, that's why we're just chillin until the crowd gets a little thicker." Maxwell formally introduced himself and his friend Grant.

"Hey, won't ya'll come inside this restaurant and have a drink with us while we wait. That is the least I could do since you hooked a brotha up with a parking spot." Max insisted. I introduced Sabrina to them as we headed inside the restaurant.

We walked in behind Max and Grant. Sabrina made it known to me that Max was hers, at least for the night. Once we hit the door of the restaurant, I was impressed. There was a line of men seated at the bar. Max greeted and introduced us to the guys. We exchanged pleasantries before Sabrina, and I took a seat at the end of the bar.

"What ya'll sippin tonight?" Max asked.

"I will have a glass of White Zinfandel." Sabrina said with a certain air of snootiness.

"I would like Grey Goose on the rocks with a lime."

"Damn girl, you doing it like that." Max asked.

"Hey, I just do what I do."

We were in the midst of man heaven. You talk about eye candy; there were beautiful, black, well-dressed, professional men everywhere. It was like looking at a million dollars in hundreds and a million dollars in fifties, which do you, choose? Both options were damn good.

Sabrina and I were the only females in the bunch, but the attention was on the upcoming football season. The guys and I sat at the bar laughing and talking while Sabrina sat flirting with them trying to see which one was gonna to take a bite. Max no longer interested in her because there were other professional ball players in the game now. This was comical to me because she looked like the ditsy cheerleader trying to catch the attention of the quarterback. I wondered if she knew how stupid she looked. I sat back surveying the lay of the land, no pun intended. I was going to choose wisely. I had to see who was for life and who was just for a night. And, if by chance I was going to get my hoe on, I had to make sure it would be with someone worth me taking off my clothes for.

Nothing really caught my attention until out the corner of my eye; I saw the reason why I busted my ass at the gym walk through the door towards us. This brotha was 6'5 about 250, wearing a denim outfit and a white rayon button down shirt.

I leaned back and whispered to Sabrina,

"Momma got this." That was girl talk for, "*this one is mine.*"

Hugs, dap, pounds, and head nods started at the other end of the bar. The closer this man got to me, the better looking he became. He finally stopped in front of me. Before Max could make the introduction, I looked this man up and down and said,

"I'm Sheridyn how you doing?"
He licked his lips, looked at me from head to toe and responded,

"Sterling. And, I'm fucking great. How are you?"
With a coy smile I replied,

"I'm damn good myself, this is my friend Sabrina." With his eyes still locked on me, he said what's up to Sabrina. I never believed in love at first sight until that moment. That brotha was working a swagger for real. After the bartender handed Sterling his drink, he nodded his head at me and walked away. He was gonna get got for real.

At that moment, I could have been bought for a nickel. Yes, I had a whole visual of the things I could do to him, I mean with him. Hell, who am I kidding, I plan to hit that tonight. He had the most kissable mouth imaginable that surrounded his straight white teeth. He was the epitome of masculinity. The scent of his cologne sent shivers down my spine and tickled me underneath. Now the tricky part of this scenario was did I want him to stay or did I just want to play? I would be satisfied if he was just a one hit wonder. The bragging rights on that would be worth wearing the label of ho in their circle. I watched Sterling while I tried to put together a game plan in my mind. I needed to figure out how I was gonna get him but make him think he was choosing me.

Talking about nothing and laughing at everything, the drinks continued to come. God knows I didn't need anything else to drink. I was a sip away from being drunk. The guys made fun of the commercial Gumbo that was being served, and I made fun of them for ordering it. After all, who comes to a ski resort in the middle of Colorado, during the summer I might add, and orders Gumbo from a bar and grill? Grant surprised me by sticking a strawberry in my mouth, I backed away from it.

"Don't act like you don't know what to do. Show me what cha working with." He said. So I inhaled deeply and sucked the strawberry tightly between my lips, sucking it out of his hand, with nothing but my lips gripping the strawberry, I hummmmed. The guys fell off their barstools like a row of dominoes in laughter. I just watched with a self-satisfied grin on my face. After they finished giving each other dap and cracking up, Sterling asked,

"What you know about that?"

"What you know about that? I know it's more than a song." I exclaimed. Max cut between Sterling and I to give me a huge hug.

"Girl, you are cool in my book, you can hang out with us anytime." I never took my eyes off Sterling, but with a flirty grin on my face, I acknowledged Max.

Sabrina sat mystified and looking uncomfortable. After the commotion died down, she leaned in and asked,

"Why did the guys think what you did was so funny?" I hate trying to explain a joke after the fact because it's never funny once you break it down, but I broke it down for her anyway.

"Back in the day, there was a song about sucking dick and it started with a woman humming on his balls. Without a response, Sabrina shouts,

"Can you eat a peach for hours?"
There was silence while the guys looked back and forth at each other in confusion.

"Because I am a sweet Georgia peach." Sabrina said.

The fellas all looked at her wondering what in the hell was she talking about. I knew what she was talking about, but I couldn't figure out how it was relevant to what was going on. The guys continued to look at each other in confusion so I said,

"That is a line from this one movie."

"Oh OK," they replied in unison. That was the politically correct way of saying, *"That was stupid and nobody gives a damn."*

At this point, everybody was partly cloudy and feeling nice. Someone suggested that we should head to the club before it got too packed. Max grabbed me again,

"You are cool people; we got to get together again." Sabrina butted in,

"We can't because I am going back to Atlanta tomorrow." No one acknowledged her.

"Ok, let's do a BBQ or something?" Sterling turned his mouth up and said,

"Girl, you can't grill?"

"Yes I can grill and can make a mean pot of greens too, now what?"
Sterling smiled and replied,

"Ok, I can make the potato salad. I can stir the potato salad for you wearing nothing but black socks and an apron." I couldn't help but notice him grinding his hips in a circular motion as he spoke. Then Max jumped on the bandwagon,

"Girl, you can't cook, what you know about greens?"

"I do more than just look good." I replied. By now, you would have thought Sabrina learned her lesson, but no, she blurts out,

"I make real good southern fried chicken."

"So does Popeye's" Sterling stated as he walked out the restaurant. I was embarrassed for her, but she didn't even realize she had just been insulted.

As soon as we entered the nightclub, we dispersed immediately. It was hot as hell in the club. I knew I would only be able to stand the heat for a minute or two. I looked around for Sterling, but he was lost in the crowd. I needed to make my move before another woman snatched his attention. The club was packed. There was no reason Sabrina couldn't meet a man and leave me alone long enough for me to holla at Sterling.

I noticed Sterling staring at me from across the room. With our eyes locked on each other, we began singing the song that was playing to each other. I was very intrigued. I walked over to him.

"Let me see if you really know how to stir...potato salad that is." I said with a smirk. Sterling held my hips and seductively replied,

"I can stir well, with quick strokes at the top to blend, or deep strokes at the bottom. The key to stirring good potato salad that is, is getting the corners. That is where all the good stuff is."

You talk about illustrative language, I was so engulfed with how he was moving, it was surprising that I heard what he said. I think he just talked me into an orgasm.

We began to move back and forth in sequence which predicated the dance. We stared into each others' eyes. Times like these, I am grateful for the short hair cut because my hair lay perfectly manicured against my head in the midst of the humidity. Wearing nothing but a thong, a long, gray, silk spaghetti strap sundress and sandals, I was comfortable. Sterling on the other hand was sweating like a slave. I unbuttoned his shirt and took it off of him. I used it to wipe the sweat from his forehead and chest. I managed to get a cheap feel. He looked like heaven dancing in that wife beater and baggy jeans. I imagined all the acrobatics I could perform with those broad shoulders.

"Let's see if you can hang."
I said as I turned my back to him and continued dancing. Sterling and I danced intimately close; I felt his breath across my shoulders. The music played and we kept a rhythm in motion. We moved in progression, our passion was conveyed with every movement.

Sterling and I were no longer moving to the beat of the music. We danced to the symphony of our beating hearts and deep breaths. We were entranced with one another. A prelude to a kiss was underway. The heat inside the club was becoming unbearable.

"Damn girl, it's hotter than fish grease in
here, I'm sweatin' liquor. Come on, let's go outside and cool off."

I was doing my happy dance inside. I didn't have the courage to have sex with him yet, but I was gonna give him a lil taste for sure. Without hesitation, Sterling grabbed my hand and we headed for the door. I love a man that takes charge of the situation.

I had no idea where we were headed, but I knew I was in capable hands. Before we made it to the parking lot, Sabrina came running out behind us.

"Where are we moving the party to?"

She was so busy trying to keep up with me; she hadn't hooked up with anyone yet. Frankly, this dance was for two; the location of the party was irrelevant to me. Before I could respond, the whole gang began to pile out the club. What I thought was going to be a romantic moment under the stars and my chance at a first kiss, turned into a round robin with the entire crew. The laughing and talking started again. This time, the crowd of men was even bigger.

As I sat on the hood of a stranger's car, Sterling and I silently flirted back and forth with each other. Out of nowhere, Sabrina grabbed Sterling's hand and walked him towards the nearby wooded area. *Houston we have a problem!* My eyebrow went up because apparently, she didn't read her "girlfriend" manual. *It's poor form to go after a man once your girl called dibs on him, especially if bonding has commenced.*

Sterling looked over his shoulder at me waiting for me to intervene, but I wouldn't. If he didn't want to go, he should have just said no. But men never walk away from the chance to witness a potential catfight. As far as Sabrina goes, I don't know why she thought she could compete with me in this arena. But for shits and grins, I will let her chase her tail and look stupid on this one. After just a few moments, Sterling and Sabrina returned from the darkness. Sterling briskly walked towards us shaking his head. I chuckled at him as soon as we reestablished eye contact.

The night progressed and Sabrina bounced around like an awkward thirteen-year-old trying to fit in. Normal women would have took note of the situation and stepped up their game, but Sabrina was not that clever. My thought was we were in the midst of man heaven, just choose one and ride it out. We were the only females amongst 11 men; this was an indication that they were looking to kick it; getting laid was not the priority. Not to say they would turn down the chance to hit, it just wasn't their focus for the evening. Sabrina had ruined my buzz, but that didn't stop me from being Sheridyn.

The guys and I continued to act a fool. The question of who was the best running back in the league erupted, and it didn't stop there. They argued about everything from who chose the best fantasy football team to who threw the most interceptions in college. I was too through when they started arguing about who was the ugliest man in the NFL. I kept thinking to myself, does any of this matter? I didn't know ESPN was looking for couch commentators. Ok, it was time to turn the attention back on me so I butted in,

"Ok, ya'll quit trippin' can't none of ya'll play ball. I bet nan one of ya'll can hold me." They laughed at me. So, I did what any woman in my position would do. I tucked my bangs behind my ear, kicked off my heels and said,

"Now what? Shall we choose teams? Shirts and skins? What? We can get a touch football game going right now. Don't let this pretty face fool you, your girl got skills. I bet I can score."

The fellas laughed as Sterling stepped to me and stood so close to me that I could taste the liquor on his breath. The way he towered over me was a true turn on. It took everything in me not to stick my tongue down his throat.

"I played basketball in college not football, so I am positive you can score." He said. He apparently hadn't realized who he was messing with.

"Momma got this; I got the wettest lay-up, it is tight, real nice, what!" I whispered.

"Check!" He replied. I took a step closer to him and said smugly,

"Understand if I suit up, there will be a game tonight. Oh yeah, I will come off the bench and score. Check!" Sterling threw his hands in the air,

"Play me or trade me coach."
Sabrina broke the mood with foolishness; she jumped up and down, shouting,

"I will be the cheerleader."

That wasn't surprising; she didn't know how to refocus attention on herself without looking like a damn fool. I am for real tired of her; she had interrupted Sterling's flirtatious melody. I turned away from Sterling and raised my hand,

"Ok who got a ball in their car? Let's do this. Or are ya'll scared a girl will rush for 50 yards during the first play?"

Max grabbed me, hugging me so tight that this time, he lifted me off the ground.

"Girl, you are cool as hell, damn girl you can kick it with us anytime. I don't know about your friend though." I couldn't do nothing but shake my head.

"You date athletes a lot don't you?" Sterling asked. That was a question from left field.

"I've dated a couple in my day, why? Are you surprised a sista know a little something about sports?"

"I knew you had to have dated athletes, because only an athlete is secure enough in himself to deal with your ass." He said as he nodded his head up and down, licking his lips. I wondered if that was a complaint or a compliment.

It was now 2 am and Sabrina had now gotten on my reserve nerve. I said good bye to the guys just so I could get away from her. Sabrina asked for their phone numbers so she could keep in touch with them. Sterling wrote his number down and gave it to me so I passed it to Sabrina. He gave me a look of disgust and wrote it down again, put it in my hand and said,

"This is for you to call me." I looked at Sabrina and back at him,

"No, I want you," he insisted.

I was so outdone with Sabrina's performance that I couldn't go back to my mom's place. I drove back to Denver, yes two hours out of the mountains at 2 am not saying two words to Sabrina. When you are kicking it with a bunch of men you have to be cool, not flighty. Finally arriving back in Denver, we slept for just a couple of hours. I damn near ran myself over getting Sabrina to the airport. More than anything, I was embarrassed at her behavior. I promised myself that she would never go anywhere else with me again. Sabrina offered me gas money as she collected her luggage; I almost wanted to give her a few dollars if she would promise not to call me again.

Chapter III

*H*eading into the office, I noticed the crumbled piece of paper with Sterling's number on it still in the ashtray of my car. This was my first time looking at the torn piece of paper since he put it in my hand a week ago. He had written his home, work, and mobile numbers with a note that read, *I don't like your friend, holla at me*. When I got to work, I decided to give him a call.

"Amcon Engineering, this is Sterling." Amcon Engineering, a Fortune 100 brother, I can work with that for sure. I thought.

"This call must be monitored for quality assurance because you know you ain't that professional. Do you know who you are talking to?" I asked.

"There is only one person I know would call me at 8 am talking trash."

"I don't know what you are talking about? I was just calling for the status of the potato salad."

"It's ready, when do you want it?"

"See, there you go. I was trying to be nice to you by checking up on a brotha but got extra work early this morning." We both chuckled.

"What's up girl, 'bout time a brotha got a phone call? The Jazz Fest was a week ago."

"Oh, look at daddy trying to keep track of a sista."

"I don't know what I'ma do with you."

"I'm sure you can think of a few things, if not, I can make a few suggestions."
Sterling chuckled on the other the end of the phone.

Talking to Sterling was like talking to an old friend. We laughed about the night we met and much to my surprise, he remembered the evening very well.

"I have to apologize to you. I was acting a fool in Winter Park. I was drunk as hell. We meet so many women that we just go with the flow." Sterling explained.

"Oh it shows that ya'll are used to women chasing ya'll. That is why I played it cool." Sterling chuckled,

"What do you mean by that?"

"What do I mean? You were trying to do it to me that night."

"You wanted me to do it to you that night." I couldn't do anything but laugh at Sterling.

"Who was that chick you were with? That girl ain't your friend; she was on one for real."

I made sure I let him know Sabrina wasn't my friend she was just someone I used to work with. He went on to say it was obvious that Sabrina doesn't get much attention. She was trying to outdo me, and the funny thing was it wasn't a competition, there were more than enough men to go around. We talked for about 15 minutes. Going over the preliminaries you know are you single, do you have kids, how old you are, etc.

Ironically, Sabrina called me later that afternoon. I told her I talked to Sterling. She ignored me. The next day, Sterling called me; he was chuckling as I answered the phone.

"Your girl called me today. I am positive that chick is crazy. She spent the majority of the conversation talking about how foreign men and white men were better in bed and that she was just too much for brothas. I don't know what the hell that was about."

"She was trying to say that she was a freak in a roundabout way. I think you should holla. You never know Sabrina might have the smack down." I said snickering to myself.

"I am for real cool on that. I'm scared to let her suck my dick." He replied. Sterling immediately diverted the conversation back on us by setting a tentative date. I must admit I was somewhat excited about seeing him again. Who am I kidding; I was counting down every minute.

I called Sabrina and let her know "*I got this.*" I knew Sterling didn't want her and she didn't like him either. For her, it was about all men should want her because she was so much better than me, so she thought. I politely told her not to call him anymore. Calling her was a big mistake. She took my call as a personal attack.

"He gave me his number. Why would he do that if he didn't want me to call?" Sabrina said with anger. I was ready to tell her about herself, but I didn't want her to think that she had something she thought I was trying to get. After I took a deep breath I said,

"If you want him, you can have him, but we are interested in each other. Besides, he was just being polite to you." After a little huffing and puffing, Sabrina hung up the phone, I never heard from her again. If I had known that was all it took to get rid of her, I would have done this a long time ago.

A couple days later, I called Sterling to iron out the details of our date; he didn't call back. I waited another day and again, still no return phone call. I threw his number away. I will only call a brotha twice, if he doesn't respond, I keep it moving. I didn't go through any changes behind him not calling, I guess I wasn't as interested as I thought I was. I allowed him to walk away without as much as a thought of why? The prelude was nice, but I guess the song wasn't composed with a hook. Time passed and a thought of Sterling never entered my mind.

It was a typical Friday night for me. I was lying on the sofa watching a movie when my mobile phone rang. I looked at the clock; it was after 11 pm. People know not to call me after 9, unless it was an emergency, if not, I'm cranky as hell.

"Hey baby whatcha doing? This is Sterling."
My first thought was Sterling who? But, as he kept talking, it dawned on me who he was. This call caught me off guard because I had not talked to him in quite awhile, I continued to listen.

"I went to the Lauren Hill concert. Now I'm at Greta's and drunk as hell, will you come get me?"

I was real confused. Why did I get a phone call "after" the concert? Why didn't I get an invitation to meet him for a drink? And, why was it my responsibility to pick his drunk ass up? After a moment of hesitation, I decided I would go pick him up.

"Ok, here I come." I got casually cute and went to Greta's to pick up Sterling. I needed to get one more gander at him before I decided to kick him off the team.

I walked through the scarcely crowded club and finally found Sterling standing at the bar. Our eyes locked, he smiled, and I smiled back at him as I migrated towards him.

"Damn, you're fine."

"Since you have the faintest idea who I am, let me save you some embarrassment, I'm Sheridyn?" I extended my arm to shake his hand. Sterling ignored my intent to shake his hand.

"Damn girl, at the Jazz Fest you looked good, but damn, I didn't know you looked this good." Sterling said as he hugged me tightly.

"Thanks for coming to get me. I ordered a couple catfish dinners for us to go." Sterling stuffed some money in my hand.

"Our food should be done, go get our food from the kitchen." All I could do was nod. When I turned to walk away, he uttered,

"Damn girl your ass looks like to cubs wrestling in a sack." I smiled, shook my head and wondered had "damn" became my new nickname. Returning with the dinners, Sterling swallowed his drink in a single gulp and escorted me out of Greta's. He insisted on me driving his car rather than riding in mine.

Sterling laid back in the passenger seat and told me where he lived. I began driving in that general direction. While driving, we approached Big Al's, which is a little hole in the wall bar. That's the spot to be if you want to party but don't want to get cute. Sterling insisted that we stop there and have a drink.

"Sterling you don't need another drink and since I am driving, I am not going to drink." Although he said ok, he continued to persuade me to stop, so I did. After parking the car, Sterling led me by the hand and to speaking to people along the way and introducing me as his girl. I accept that he was on one, but I was not feeling him in the least. At this point, the chances of me becoming his girl are slim to none.

The moment we entered the club, Sterling walked straight to the bar and ordered a drink. I refused to let him buy me a drink. Sterling looked at me and said,

"Damn girl you are fine as hell, baby in real life you are fine." Sterling started running his fingers through my hair and rubbing my face. I looked up only to see Rod, my ex-boyfriend glaring at us. Rod and I left things undone and this was his first time seeing me since we broke up. Rod was the first man that I ever loved, and his claim to fame was that he was also the first man that ever broke my heart. I never considered myself "Hellava" but I never knew rejection or experienced heartache. That shit hurts!

It had been almost 9 nine months since Rod and I broke up but it was still tender. Heartache is like an echo and time passes the pain is present but fades over time. For the first few months, after our breakup, all I did was cry. I didn't know when people said love hurts that you could physically feel the pain of heart break. I sure as hell felt it. I vowed to myself that I would never let a man hurt me like that again.

Rod staring at me was a little uncomfortable. I didn't know what to expect from him or Sterling. I pretended I didn't see Rod. The more I tried to casually resist Sterling's advances of affection, the more he complimented me by caressing my hair and face. He finished his drink and we headed to the door. Rod was obviously angry, but we left the club before any drama popped off.

Finally, Sterling and I left Big Al's and headed to his place. He invited me inside his apartment to eat my catfish with him. I agreed. Once inside, I performed the initial check of his apartment, looking for the signs of another woman. I was surprised this was definitely a bachelor's pad. I really don't think a woman or should I say a permanent woman had been there in quite awhile. The furniture didn't match, there were no pictures on the walls, but there was $3000 worth of stereo and television equipment. And you guessed correctly, there was a game station in the middle of the floor.

Sterling brought us some lemonade in two slightly faded plastic collector's cups, the ones they give out at the fast-food restaurants. We ate and watched television in silence. Sterling passed out on the sofa before he finished eating. I put his food in the refrigerator and found us a couple of blankets. I threw one blanket over him, and I laid in the middle of the floor with the other one. I didn't get in the bed because Sterling might have woken up during the night and thought I was inviting him to get some ass.

About 6 am, I woke Sterling up to take me back to my car. We engaged in idle chitchat while we drove. He was still drunk. When we arrived at the parking lot outside of Greta's, he kissed me on the cheek. Ladies and gentlemen, that was the end. The curtains were on my fantasy of Sterling. He was just a drunk trying to get laid. I would not be surprised if he called me because I was the first woman, he was able to reach as he scrolled through the list of names listed in his cell phone. Alcoholism is a true turn off for me. I never called him back and he didn't call me either. I still have no idea what that night was about. I was disappointed because he could have been a whole wonderful boo.

Chapter IV

The ladies and I stopped at Greta's for an after work drink. Shortly after we arrived, Sterling and his crew walked in. Sterling noticed me immediately; he walked towards me with a smile. He hugged me like we were old friends. Sterling introduced me to the crew, and then offered to buy me another drink. The conversation was light; we mingled and got the party started. I couldn't hold it in any longer. I looked up at Sterling and said,

"Come here, real close." With a big kool-aid grin on his face, Sterling complied.

"Ok, what was that episode 6 months ago all about? Let me tell you about yourself."

After I reminded him about that evening, he laughed in shame and said,

"To be honest with you, I have no idea why I called you or better yet, where I even found your number. I am so embarrassed. Can I buy you dinner later this week as a token of good faith?"

"If you pass out this time, I just might take advantage of your innocence." I smirked.

"Hell, with a threat like that, I will get drunk on purpose. Just know that there is nothing innocent about me." Sterling replied with a little chuckle.

Sterling and I exchanged numbers again. If he was interested, he would call me, I thought. If not, no love lost. I just hoped if he called, he would be sober this time. I was not as attracted to him as much as I was. Much to my surprise, Sterling called the next day and we set a date. He even called back the day before to confirm our date.

It had been about 3 days since the last time Sterling and I saw each other. We decided to meet directly after work at Hops. Things were very light and casual. We watched the basketball game in the bar and got to know each other. I was impressed, he was quite intelligent. We shared the same views on social and political issues; we also had identical family values. No matter what we talked about, we kept revisiting the night we met and laughed. We compared our favorite restaurants and movies. We seemed to be reading from the same sheet of music.

Sterling suggested that we get a table versus sitting at the bar. I think he wanted to create a more intimate setting. We ordered dinner and talked nonstop. We exchanged war stories about our past relationships and of course we laughed. We agreed that neither one of us was interested in being in a relationship. We were mutually interested in each other, but neither one of us wanted to be the first to express what we were feeling. It was apparent Sterling was a player and I was still healing from my last relationship. The thought of us being a couple was the furthest thing from our minds, while sex was on the forefront of our minds.

I was surprised to hear Sterling's story. He was originally from Chicago and had been living in Denver since high school. What made his story so interesting was that 3 of his best childhood friends were well known NBA players. I listened to him talk about how they spent nights at each others' house from grade school to high school and all balled together. Sterling talked about how he was disappointed that they kept in contact with him but not each other. He felt they let team rivalry disband their friendship. I listened attentively, but I thought he was lying, so I didn't even ask why he didn't go pro with his boys. There was no need for Sterling to try to impress me with tall tales because my sexual desire for him was already present and accounted for.

We tried to redirect our focus from the obvious topic at hand, which was *when were we gonna get busy!* We pretended that we were deeply engulfed in the game. For the life of me, I couldn't tell you who was playing. Basketball was a great façade. He was shocked that I knew about sports. I knew the game, players, and voiced an intelligent prediction about who was destined for the playoffs.

"I guess you weren't just showing off at the Jazz Fest, you do know a little somethin somethin."

"I strive to be well rounded. Besides, dating is like basketball, there are starters, substitutes, and those that are waiting to be drafted." Sterling nodded at me,

"That's very true. When is your agent gonna send over some game footage." I smiled,

"You might see some highlights tonight."

"Sheridyn, I am interested in your lay-up." I think I would throw myself off a curb if this dance wasn't worth all that it is building up to be.

I believe we had overstayed our welcome. More than two hours had passed, and we were still camped out at the restaurant, but neither one of us wanted to say goodbye. We finally exited the restaurant to find it snowing outside. This was typical weather in Denver. We have a saying here, *"if you don't like the weather here, wait 5 minutes it'll change."* Sterling suggested that I sit in his car while mine warmed up. He was trying to be a gentleman, but I knew he just wanted to be alone with me for a moment. That feeling was more than mutual. You can definitely tell this was a first date. We were both tense and awkward.

"Sheridyn I want to kiss you." Before I could respond, Sterling grabbed me by the back of the head and gave me a hot, wet, passionate kiss that never ended. Simultaneously, we began caressing and undressing one another. Never unlocking lips, I slipped my hand into his pants where I found him erect. I began to stroke him while he made his way into my pants.

"Damn girl, you are so wet. I want you now." He whispered. Before I knew it, that kiss was the prelude to what I would consider the best orgasm that I had in at least a year. Partially undressed, I continued to stroke him until, he came in my hand. Sterling looked at me and said,

"Wow!"

I didn't know what to say. He continued to gently slide his fingers back and forth across my most sensitive areas. I tensed up and moaned softly as I released. He continued kissing me on my neck, he was still erect. We were silenced by the amazement of what had just happened. Some first kiss.

Sterling invited me to go home with him. I reminded him that his sister and her kids were at his place for the week. Going to my house while my children were there was not an option either. I guess this meant we were gonna have to go our separate ways. I kissed him on the forehead. He grabbed me and excitedly kissed me again. The passion rose.

"Ok, I gotta go for real this time." I immediately fastened and readjusted my clothes. I quickly gathered my composure and got out of his car. Before I got out of the parking lot, Sterling called my cell phone,

"What was that? I guess you are damn good" he said.

"I think this was the residual affects of our first time meeting each other." Neither one of us really knew what to say, wow just kept coming out of Sterling's mouth, I couldn't help but chuckle a little and ask him,

"Why do you keep saying that?"

"Nothing like that has ever happened to me. I still can't believe I came in your hand like that." Neither one of us had never experienced anything like that before, especially without penetration. Being coy I said,

"It was the liquor."

"Liquor my ass. Damn girl!" I don't know why I found being with Sterling amusing, but I did. We talked until my phone died. After I got home and cleaned myself up, I called him back. Sterling apologized for letting things go so far and expressed how much he enjoyed the kiss.

For the next several weeks. Sterling and I played phone tag and could not nail down a date to save our lives. I was busy with my children's activities, and he was just busy. Finally, I suggested that I should come over after I got the children in bed, and I would bring a movie. It was standard practice for me not to entertain male company when my children were home, besides, his place was more convenient. My children were old enough to stay alone and since I had to be at work the next morning, I knew I wouldn't stay out too late.

After putting the children to bed, I grabbed a movie and headed to Sterling's apartment. He greeted me at the door with a hug and a kiss on the forehead. Sterling's apartment was the same as it was the first time, I was there almost a year earlier.

"My dad is home so let's go to my room."
I thought it was a little strange that his father was living with him, but I didn't ask why.

Fully clothed Sterling and I laid in bed and watched the movie. Sterling took a psychological approach towards the film. He explained that he liked lions because of their masculinity and dominance. He pointed out that is why he had them on the walls of his room. We laughed at the same scenes and enjoyed the movie as if it was our first time watching it. Sterling never made an advance.

The movie ended. I sat up to put on my shoes while the movie was rewinding. Sterling agreed that we should end the night early because he had to be at work at 7 am also. Just as I stood up, Sterling grabbed me by the back of the head, kissed me, and laid me back on the bed. As he passionately kissed me, he rubbed his hands all over my body. Before I knew it, we were both undressed and l was lying underneath him. We never breached the kiss or the embrace. The room was silent. The harmonious sounds of enthusiasm echoed through the air.

Sterling gently kissed my body. He nibbled on my neck. He moved down my neck to suck my nipples, he slid his fingers between my legs.

"Girl you are so damn wet I want you now." He muttered as he rose off me and pulled me deeper into the bed. Sterling separated my legs and licked me intimately. My legs began to quiver, and he became more zealous about licking me and sucking my nectar. I tensed up and my legs trembled, I released and let go of my first orgasm. He knew I had climaxed. Sterling quit licking me and nibbled his way back up my body.

We continued to kiss, I felt Sterling slide himself inside of me. Sterling was still for a moment and towered over me, looking directly into my eyes, as to receive permission to continue. I lifted my leg up to allow him to move in deeper. I wrapped my hands around his back, and we began to make love. Deep, hot, and passionately, we moved in harmony with a certain air of familiarity. I rubbed his chest, he groaned mildly. I lifted my head off the bed, firmly closed my lips around his nipples and sucked as he continued his stroke. We made love as if we've intimately known each other forever. We massaged, kissed and caressed each other with motions of love. I was breathless.

After reaching our pinnacle, we laid next to each other in silence and utter amazement. Sterling kissed me on the top of my head and went to the bathroom. Immediately after the toilet flushed, I heard the shower running. While he was in the bathroom, I put my clothes on. When he returned from the bathroom, I was dressed with my keys in my hand.

"You don't have to leave."

"I better go because it is a school night." This time WOW kept playing in my mind. I have had my share of good dick; but damn! I didn't know if this was the beginning or the end. I actually felt awkward because he jumped in the shower immediately after we were done having sex. What was that all about, I wondered? Am I a bootie call already?

I still wasn't sure what I thought about the first night together. I didn't want to be the person to make the first call *afterwards* so I just wondered. Although, I really wanted to see him again and perhaps hit that one more time, I didn't call. At this point, I didn't know if he was going to be a one hit wonder or a regular. It's been a few days since our night together. I thought about him and how good the sex was. I anxiously anticipated his call, but I was also prepared not to hear from him again.

Wrapping up my workday, my office telephone rang.

"Hey baby how are you doing?" It was Sterling.

"What time do you get off work?"

"Now, why?"

"I need a huge favor, will you pick me up from the office, my car is in the shop and I need a ride home?"

"I was in the process of packing up when you called so I am on my way." He was surprised that I agreed to pick him without hesitation.

"Thanks for doing this for me; by the way, I am here by myself." I assumed he said that so I would hurry up. But when I didn't respond, he said it again,

"I'm here by myself." That time I caught what he meant.

"What are you trying to say?" I asked.

"I am not trying to say anything; I am just saying I'm here by myself."

"Is that information or an invitation?" He chuckled and said,

"You call it." After he gave me directions, I left the office.

Sterling and I worked on opposite ends of the city. I had plenty of time to think of a strategy to take advantage of the fact that he was at the office alone. I figured he was telling me he wanted to get him a lil somethin at the office. I arrived at his job about 45 minutes later. I entered his office to find him alone and on the phone. He nodded at me and continued talking. I straddled him as he sat in his plush, leather swivel office chair. I started loosening his tie and I unbuttoned his shirt. I kissed his neck and nibbled on his ear. He indicated he was on the phone with his brother Derrick and to give him a minute. Even with his hand gripping my butt, he continued his conversation as if I wasn't there.

"Are you going to talk on the phone or attend to the matters at hand?" I asked. He nodded at me but stayed engaged in conversation. That meant I needed to turn up the fire.

I got off his lap and stood on top of his mahogany desk. Peering over him, I slowly removed one item of clothing at a time. Sterling leaned back in his chair to enjoy the strip tease show. I had definitely grasped his attention. Finally, standing in nothing but heels and a g-string, I began to dance alluring and sexy.

"Man I gotta go, there is an ass naked woman standing on my desk. Dude, there is nothing but ass in my face." Sterling placed the phone next to my butt. Confused I asked,

"What are you doing?"

"Derrick wanted to hear what your ass had to say." We laughed as he hung the phone up.

Sterling pulled me off the desk on top of him in the chair. We began to kiss eagerly, and I finished undressing him. Throwing his clothes across the room, knocking everything off his desk but the computer, we began to make love on his desk. He picked me up and sat me in his chair with my legs extended wide, he started licking me closely. The feeling of his soft, warm tongue fluttering across my clit caused me to climax quickly. He began to gently suck my juices as I came. I released hard and shivered in ecstasy.

I got off the chair and placed him in my mouth and sucked firmly. My actions caught him off guard, because he signaled me to stop immediately. I got off my knees and began to ride him. I moved up and down with him inside of me, he ran his fingers up my back and through my hair. He wrapped his arms under my arms and pushed himself deeper inside of me. The way he passionately nibbled across my shoulders and sucked on my breasts only caused me to want him more.

Sterling held me tight in his arms, stood up and laid me on the floor. He continued stroking deep inside of me. My legs rested in his arms. Without so much as a simple gesture, we got off the floor and continued to make love on every imaginable surface in his office. Finally, standing up against the wall with Sterling behind me, I bent over and grabbed his ankles. I began to bounce my butt up and down. That raised the level of passion that was already escalating. Sterling began to squeal. Discretion was not on our agenda and the scenery promoted even more of an erotic setting.

"I'm not ready to cum yet." He whispered as he pulled himself out of me. With my back to him, he slightly nibbled across my shoulders and neck. He had a tight grip on my hair with one hand and slid the other hand between my legs. I slid my hand over his hand and touched myself. Once my fingertips were covered in juices, I stuck my fingers in his mouth and began to kiss him through our fingers. Now that really turned him on.

Sterling laid me on the floor for our climatic ending. Sterling's stroke was strong and vigorous. He yelled and released. Almost out of breath, he rolled onto his back pulling me on top of him. Lying on his chest, I looked at him and smiled.

"Wow, look what you did." He said. Why was I to blame? *He was the one that had said he was at the office alone.*

Our cuddling was soon interrupted by the sound of the evening janitorial service cleaning the office next door. All we could do is look at each other and laugh. I'm butt naked and he was wearing nothing but his black dress socks. Articles of clothes were sprawled across his office. There were pants on the artificial tree, a tie on the chair, a shirt flung over the file cabinet. It was like a scavenger hunt trying to get dressed. I don't consider myself a prude or anything but couldn't believe I did something like this, much less with someone who wasn't my man. I hope he doesn't think this is something I do on the regular. I don't even know why I did it this time. I was a little embarrassed, but not in the least regretful.

We got dressed and discreetly left the office. There were no words to describe what had just happened; we smirked back and forth at one another as if each of us was taking credit for what we had done. Arriving at his apartment, Sterling gave me a peck on the lips.

"Thanks for picking me up, I appreciate it and boy did I enjoy it. Call me when you get home so that I know you made it safely." He said.

"You better go before we get started again, besides I need to get home and check on the children." He gave me an endearing peck on the lips and got out the car. We both knew if he hadn't gotten out of the car, the trumpet of *let the games begin* would have sounded and we would have been at it again.

Over the next several months, Sterling and I continued to date. He introduced me to his father. His father was elderly and had a great sense of humor. He was self-sufficient but he needed partial supervision. I don't think his father distinguished me from any other woman Sterling might have brought home, never calling me by name, but nonetheless, he was still pleasant and polite to me. One evening, I was visiting Sterling and his father actually came out of his room to talk to me.

One daring night, Sterling and I decided that we would take some personal pictures, if you know what I mean. I teased Sterling that I was going to blackmail him, for some reason, he thought it would be a good idea to share this with his father.

"Pops, can you believe this, she is sitting in our house threatening to blackmail me?"

"You probably did something to deserve it, I just hope she is willing to share the money she is gonna get from you." I snickered.

"Pops that's cold you supposed to have my back."

"I do but getting a couple of dollars is good too." Sterling was surprised how his father responded to me trying to blackmail him.

Whenever I came to visit Sterling, I always brought a movie with me. In some twisted way, the movie was foreplay. Something reminiscent of the first time we made love. The sex was unbelievable; the passion was turned up a notch with each encounter. Our bodies molded together as one. We never discussed what we liked or disliked sexually. We never talked about the love we made together, but the danger was we never defined our relationship either. We just went with the tempo and rode the vibe. In some way, our lovemaking became a competition of who could make who feel the best. We both were passionate about winning.

Our conversation was the most stimulating part of our relationship. As we laid in bed, Sterling and I had our most intimate conversations. He was naked, not just physically. We would have debates on relationships, interracial dating, racism, gender communication, etc. The topic didn't matter, we stayed in constant dialogue. I thought Sterling was the best thing since sliced bread because of the respect he held for his mother and his love for children. His intellect moved me, he spoke with conviction and he possessed a thirst for knowledge.

Sterling was with his last girlfriend for 7 years and he loved her two sons as if they were his own. He told me how he taught them the virtues that a good man should possess. He believed a man should always have money in his pocket. I knew he would be a great role model for my children. In fact, I developed a strong respect and admiration for him. He possessed old fashioned values that were a lost commodity in men, especially young men. I knew he would protect my daughter, discipline my sons, and provide for me. I would have been proud if my boys grew up to be the type of man that Sterling was.

Sterling wanted his first child to be a girl and name her Taylor that is his middle name. He said that would love her so much her mother's beauty would pale in comparison to her. Sterling emphasized that he would not have any kids until he got married, because he wanted to be a part of his child's everyday life. He held being a father in high esteem. He went as far as to say, if his marriage ended in divorce, he would fight for custody because he refused to be a part time father. Sterling had so many traits that reminded me of my father. Sterling was definitely a keeper. I wonder if he thought the same of me.

"I love kids, but people treat their kids any kind of way. Let me tell you about this one chick I was cool with. Me and like three of my homeboys were over there kicking it one night, you know drinking and shit. We all passed out on the sofa, chair, and floor, whatever. The next morning, we woke up. Her two kids were sitting on the floor eating cereal and watching cartoons. Man, that shit was ill. We never met her kids before and they woke up to find four different brothas asleep in their house. The kicker was that she had a man. Them kids didn't need to see all that. That was so disrespectful." He explained.

"I agree with you, but why would ya'll kick it like that knowing she had kids?" I asked.

"She didn't respect her house, so we didn't respect her."

"That is the very reason that I don't introduce men to my children until I know that we might be together for a minute. That is why I don't entertain male company at my house when my little people are home."

Sterling asked me if I wanted any more children. I was a little apprehensive to answer the question because I had never told Sterling that I couldn't have children. I guess we should have had this conversation before we became sexually active. I wonder if he knew because up to this point, we never discussed birth control or practiced safe sex. I guess this was as good of time as any to fess up. What was the worse that could happen?

"I have always wanted 5 children. Unless I marry someone that already has children, I will only have the three that I got already. My tubes were tied 5 years ago." Sterling shrugged off my response. I couldn't tell if that meant he didn't care, or if the fact that I could not have children disqualified me from being the soloist in his orchestra.

When it came to making love to Sterling, I was completely uninhibited, there were no holds barred. We never took foreplay lightly. He made sure he gave my body a tongue-lashing before he went in. Sterling made sure he touched every inch of my body. This particular night before the movie ended, Sterling began to passionately nibble on my neck, run his fingers through my hair and pulling it lightly. We undressed each other and moved to the beat of our hearts. The musical sounds of our lovemaking were always at a fanatical tempo. We seemed to always make love like it was going to be our last time. We were guaranteed to have at least two orgasms before it was all said and done. Every effort was used in our lovemaking process. While Sterling stroked, we caressed, and nibbled simultaneously. Damn!

No matter how good the loving was, we managed to take it up an octave. When we made love, it was always harmonic, daring, and different. One evening, Sterling had a wild hair up his ass this particular night. As the prelude to making love began, Sterling pulled my thong off with his teeth. He moved back up my body nibbling every inch of the way, he grabbed my hands. When he reached my face, he held my arms over my head and tied my hands to the headboard with my thong. Peering over me Sterling said,

"Now what? Whatcha gon' do now?" Apparently, he still didn't know who he was dealing with.

"Ok, don't start something you aren't in position to finish." I said devilishly.

"I am going to show you what I can do, and you can't stop me." He whispered as he moved down my body. Sterling grabbed my ankles, twisted my legs up to my earlobes.

"I'm not scared. What?" I said candidly,

"Oh yeah watch this!" He moved deep inside my legs and began to scrupulously lick me, smooth and gently while sucking my clit. I started to quiver as I reached my sexual crescendo. Sterling wrapped his arms over my legs and held my shoulders. I was pinned to the bed. I could not move. He buried his entire face between my legs. I started to release the best orgasm conceivable; I experienced the vibrations of multiple orgasms. Before one orgasm ended, I started cumming again. With my hands tied to the bed and my body pinned, I was at his mercy.

I was not gonna let him have me open and sprung. I couldn't take it anymore; I broke my hands free and wiggled from underneath him. I laid him down, got on top of him and began to ride. I hopped onto my feet and clinched his tip inside of me and began to pop fast. That drove him wild.

"Now what?" I said. Sterling clinched me tight pulling me down so that all of him was inside of me; I threw his hands off me and said,

"No not yet." With him still inside of me, I turned around, grabbed his ankles and continued riding.

"Damn, girl, damn." he yelled as he reached his peak. Sterling couldn't control it, he screamed as he came inside of me. His toes pointed straight up then curled. I guess that meant the score was tied now, I thought to myself as he pulled me to his chest and held me close.

Chapter V

Some people have too much time on their hands when they are at the office, so they spend their day forwarding emails and chain letters. I usually delete them without reading them. I received a forward that apparently had been floating around in cyber space. The email implied that this white woman supposedly wrote a letter to a black, female magazine stating that brothas thought black women were needy, evil, uneducated bitches, and carried too much drama. In a nutshell, black women had nothing to offer him. Somehow, the email was sent to both Sterling and I. I read the email while replies from all directions started pouring in. The women were chatting back and forth in outrage on how they thought this white woman was out of line and offensive. They were ready to beat down this nameless faceless woman.

I had to put a stop to the madness, so I joined the email conversation. I typed my response. *Whether the story is true or not is irrelevant, but we need to examine a few things. First, why are you mad at her for repeating what some ignorant brotha told her, probably to boost his ego and get laid? Other cultures that date outside of their race say that they prefer other races. You never hear them bash their own race or give up dating their race because of some idiot they may have encountered. Where as black folks do the textbook stereotypical thing and disgrace their race.*

Secondly, if you have to be mad at a white woman, you should be mad at the white woman that fought for equal rights for women. While women won rights in the workplace, the black family was destroyed. Black families never had issues about who was supposed to be in what role. Historically, black men haven't been respected in the workplace and with the feminine rights movement; they were put in a position to no longer be respected at home either. Black women, its ok to be independent but we have to let a man be a man.

My thought was I believe all people have a disgraceful group within their race, but when I see a person that has issues with everyone they date, I advise them to look at the common denominator. If the same thing is wrong with everybody that you encounter, then you have to take a gander at yourself. Why do you keep choosing the same type of person? Or better yet, are you giving what you are expecting to receive? And as my granny always said, *you can't fish in a catfish farm expecting to catch anything other than catfish.* I ruffled some feathers with my email response, but no one had a valid argument against my statements.

Later that evening, Sterling and I went on a date. The main topic of conversation was the email and my response.

"I totally agree with you, there are very distinct roles between men and women and most black women today won't acknowledge that. Gender roles are complimentary not competing. When I was with my ex, my money was direct deposited into the bank and she paid all the bills. I am a man; I don't suppose to write checks. I had cash in my pocket for whatever I needed, and she handled the shit at home. In fact, after we broke up, I showed up on her doorstep with my hand full of bills and my checkbook. My job is to take care of my woman and it's her job to take care of the house." Sterling exclaimed.

Ladies and gentlemen, we have a winner, I shared his mindset. Growing up every other Friday, my dad went to the bank, withdrew his personal allowance and my stepmother paid all the bills. If there was an expense outside of the normal household budget like when we had to buy a new freezer, we went as a family and bought it.

"There are things I don't think I am supposed to do because I am a lady. I am independent and I know how to get done whatever I need to have done. However, there are just some things I don't think I am supposed to do like mow lawn, shovel snow, take out trash, or wash my car when a man is present. By the same token, I don't think you as a man should cook, clean, or take care of domestic duties. Of course, there are exceptions, but if two people are doing one job, then it means the other job isn't covered or it's only being done half assed." I replied.

The destruction of the black family began when women thought they didn't need a man, thus removing the authority, provision and protection from the home which lead to broken values. Women began getting rid of their men as if they were 8 tracks, never considering how their choice would impact children and ultimately a generation.

"The way I look at is if one sex was supposed to do it all, we wouldn't have two. Not to say either gender shouldn't know how to do everything, there are just some things that our genetic makeup tells us we aren't supposed to do. Think about this, I know how to type, but I was hired to work in sales. Better yet, if we both are on fries, then nobody is working the cash register. The key ingredient in the recipe is that both entities are aware of their role and recognize the need of the other role." Sterling stated.

Boy, his intellect was turning me on. I could have just ripped his clothes off and done him right then. Instead, I chose to reply,

"It amazes me when I meet women that say they don't need a man. I will admit I do, the family unit does. Not because I am weak or dependent, but because I can teach my son to be a good person, but only a man can teach him to be a good man. Only a man can show my daughter how a man should love her. As a lady, I need protection and provision. We wonder why so many boys are growing up sexually confused when they have never seen a man shave or tie a tie, but they have watched their mothers put on make up and pantyhose." Sterling shook his head in agreement.

"When a woman is put in a position to provide rather than nurture that leaves the child missing out on what will shape him or her."

"See, that is what I am talking about, men and women are designed to compliment each other not compete against each other." I repeated.

I had to play it cool. The na na was on fire though. I was ready to ask the waitress for the tab and go do it in the car and again once we got home. I didn't want him to think that sex was the only reason I came around, although it kept me coming back. Sterling was tall, handsome, intelligent, well dressed, and sexy. I can go on and on. The bottom line was I really wanted this man. I was interested in being exclusive with him.

Chapter VI

There was only a hand full of blacks at the company I worked for, so we tried to make it a point to at least "look like" there was a united front among us. We spoke daily, even though we really didn't know anything about each other except we were black and worked at the same company. One morning, I walked between the cubicles that monopolized the department, and ran into Jessica. Jessica was a bi-racial, slightly overweight girl that worked in another department. She worked hard to prove how "black" she was. She was amusing at times because she was cool, but just tried a little too hard to fit in. Her mother worked as an executive with us, which meant Jessica thought she was even that much more important.

"Hey girl what's up? Do you know a guy named Sterling Jacobs?" Now that was a question outta nowhere. Jessica and I had worked together for six months and we never talked personal before. I am personable but damn personal, especially when it came to dealing with people in the office.

"Yes, I know him."

"Oh, I noticed your name on an email forward that he sent out and I wonder if you were the same Sheridyn. He and I used to kick it." Jessica said.

"Oh, ok." I replied. That wasn't the response she was waiting for, but I never volunteer information. She should have asked me specifically what she wanted to know.

Jessica was not a person that you wanted to know your business. She told everybody's business. I only dealt with her in passing and she still managed to tell me the business of all her friend's that I had never even met. So I can only imagine what she would feed them about me. Jessica was always in search of the juicy fruit.

Happy Hour on Thursday nights at the Bombay was the place to be. I usually dodged "social" events with the office staff, but after saying no so many times, the girls in the office started hassling me about being a party pooper. I finally decided to go since I had run out of excuses of why I couldn't. As my luck would have it, I would show up when no one but Jessica went. Jessica was cool, but she was definitely someone you needed to feed with a long handle spoon.

The Bombay was a restaurant and dance club. Prominent hotels and businesses surrounded the Bombay. The crowd was mostly traveling professionals, staying in the neighboring hotels and corporate employees that stopped in for a quick drink and exchange business cards before going home. There was not much eye candy that evening, but there were a few options available. Jessica and I had a drink, absorbed the scenery, and talked about work. Everything was status quo. Times like this I was grateful for the gift of gab. I was able to control the conversation and make sure I was not the topic of the evening.

Jessica and I both noticed Sterling, his brother Derrick and their friend Pete walk in. Sterling hesitantly smiled after seeing Jessica and I at the table together. After the initial shock wore off, he walked to our table. He gave me a hug and a kiss on the cheek. This was the way he typically greeted me so it was all good so far. I watched as he hugged Jessica, their hug was cold and distant. I spoke to Derrick and Pete. When Derrick leaned over to hug Jessica, she loudly whispered,

"He is so busted." I don't know what she meant by that, but I was interested in seeing how this evening was going to play out. Sterling and I had not defined our relationship so I had no reason to be upset, yet. In fact, he was looking damn good to me in those slacks and button down. After another Goose; I think we might be going home together. I am positive he would ditch the fellas to make it happen. Immediately after the guys found their own table, Jessica started in.

"I don't know what Sterling is trying to pull and why he's trying to be such a player. He's gonna walk up and hug both of us like nothing's wrong. Girl that is why I left his sorry ass alone! He ain't even the kind of man I want in my life. How is he grown and still living with his father? Men today ain't shit they are always trying to play a sista!" Jessica expressed. It was clear that she was pissed off.

I continued sipping my drink trying to figure out what had Sterling done that warranted such animosity from Jessica. Before I could get a word in edgewise, Jessica kept going.

"We were supposed to hook up after that party I invited you to next Friday, I'm not giving his sorry ass the time of day." Jessica concluded. My eyebrow rose as she talked, could she be the reason why Sterling and I wasn't a couple. She got a couple things going for her, but she couldn't hold a candle to me.

I knew how much time I spent with Sterling so if Jessica was it, she wasn't getting much playing time at all. I needed to know who the point guard was and who the substitute was. Jessica just said she left him alone, so why is she trippin? I liked Sterling and all however he is not Big Dick Willie. There was no way that I was going to continue kicking it with him if he was kicking it with her. There was not gonna be any collar popping around these here parts because he is hitting two women that know about each other.

"Sheridyn, I don't think Sterling is where he should be in life. You know he don't have a real job and he lives in an apartment with his father. You have to admit that shit ain't even cool" This was typical Jessica. She pulled out a superior card when it was convenient. Now that she knows Sterling and I know each other, all of a sudden, he ain't shit. I just sat peeping game. She just said she was going to hook up with him next week, but then she said he was sorry. That's what confused me. I guess everything was sorry but his dick.

I was ready to go home because I finally had enough of *Why is Sterling sorry for $200 Alex*. And watching Sterling out the corner of my eye was going to get him got for real. I am a sucker for a well-dressed man. This was my first time seeing Sterling in business attire in a long time. *Damn* was the only thing that could describe how good he was looking. Sippin on a drink only added fuel to my fantasy. Jessica and I weren't talking about a damn thing anyway. I had tuned her out a while ago; she wasn't going to change my opinion of Sterling. One good thing about having children, they were an automatic out in any situation.

"Girl let's go, you know I gotta go home and cook for my babies." I said to Jessica with a sigh. She agreed because she was so angry with Sterling. Protocol warranted us to say goodbye to the guys on our way out the door. Jessica glared at Sterling and said goodbye to Pete and Derrick. I smiled at Sterling and he nodded at me with a grin on his face. Jessica was so worried that I was going to linger at the Bombay with Sterling and the fellas; she sat in her car and fiddled around until I pulled off. Jessica thought she was all that, but she was concerned about me. I love it.

After I got home, got the kids situated, and relaxed, Sterling called me laughing,

"What's up baby, so what did Jessica have to say? I know she was talking shit; she has been blowing my phone up. I didn't know ya'll were friends."

"Damn, you didn't tell me you were putting it down like that! You know that you are all kinds of sorry, no good, player, nothing so and so's. We aren't friends, we just work together. She asked me about you the other day."

"Why did she ask you about me?"

"Because she saw my name on a forward you sent. She kept hoping that I would spill my guts, but I have nothing to say to her about you. You aren't my man so what can I say? I am just mad you giving it to her like that. Am I just getting a little man's portion of loving or what?"

"Trust me, it ain't even like that." He answered.

Don't get it twisted I was boiling inside. I am selfish and didn't want to share him with nobody, especially sharing with someone that couldn't appreciate him, but I had to keep it light. See, we weren't supposed to have feelings. We were just spending time together. I wanted him to be my man, but he didn't push the envelope, so I didn't either. I was supposed to be the object of his affection and then to find out he messed with Jessica, was a turn off. I know good and hell well that she ain't popping it like me. So, he must like something about her, but what? I was barely paying attention to what Sterling had to say. I was running the evening's events through my head over and over again. By the end of the conversation, Sterling invited me over. As bad as I needed some, I didn't go. I guess I was punishing him for messing with Jessica. He needed to think about what he had and what he was at risk of losing.

For the next few days, Jessica became like a fly bugging the hell out of me while I was trying to eat. In her mind, Sterling became some sort of common bond between us. Everything became about Sterling. One afternoon, she came to my office and said,

"You know that is your boy's girl?" Looking puzzled

"Who?" I replied as I shook my head in confusion. She pointed at a picture of Nia Long depicted on the magazine on my desk.

"What boy?"

"Sterling, you know he loves him some Nia Long." Oh, ck I thought. Jessica found a way to bring up Sterling's name every chance she could, dropping little tidbits of information, hoping I would bite. Perhaps she was trying to establish in her mind that she wasn't just a bootie call, she "knows" him. She was still trying to figure out who I was to him. Frankly, it was getting on my damn nerves.

It was Friday and time to go to the party that Jessica had been talking about for weeks. I was reluctant to go, but I could only imagine the stories she would tell about me to the people at the party. I got as fine as I could and went anyway because I knew it was highly probable that I would see Sterling before the night was over.

Boy I now know what my mother meant when she said *always follow your first mind*. Once again "Sterling" was the topic of conversation,

"You know Sterling and I was going to hook up after the party until I found out about you." Jessica recounted. She went as far as introducing me to the other women at the party as *"this is the girl that helped me bust Sterling."* I believe in ignoring ignorance but this was too much. Bust him how? Bust him doing what?

Besides, Jessica's general presence being bothersome, I was enjoying the ladies only party that was complete with a male stripper and jello shots. I sat debating mentally what I was going to do about this Jessica and Sterling situation. Should I even care about them? If he wants me in his life he will have to show it, because I think I am all that, therefore jocking a brotha was out of the question.

Now that the beefcakes were gone, it was time to move the party to Greta's. I broke the number one party rule; I didn't drive my own car, which meant there was not an accessible escape plan if I needed one. I rode with Jessica and her cousin. Greta's was one of those spots that you are guaranteed to run into someone you know. As I made it through the crowd meeting and greeting people, I saw some guy I knew from back in the day. He bought me a drink like I needed another one, but I was already on a roll so why quit? I was partly cloudy and the last thing I needed was to be unaware of my surroundings. There was no way I could have stomached Jessica this long if I was sober. I still don't remember that man's name but we took a picture and sat chatting.

Jessica found me seated next to the dance floor. She interrupted my conversation with *random dude,*

"You need to come upstairs Sterling is tripping."

"About what, why should I care?" Some people just don't get it. I only care about the things I care about and right now, I didn't care about her or Sterling. I was chillin'.

"Sheridyn just come up stairs." She insisted. I saw that she was not going away, so I followed her upstairs because she was aggravating the hell out of me. At the top of the stairs, Sterling was in the center of a huddle of men. He noticed me immediately and smiled. I smiled, licked my lips and said,

"How are you sir?" As usual, he was a sight for sore eyes. Sterling stopped talking to the guys mid sentence.

"Sterling your ass is drunk." Jessica yelled. Sterling stepped to me with a seductive look and said,

"You used to take care of me when I was drunk." At that moment, no one existed but Sterling and I.

"I ain't starting point guard anymore; I have been dropped to the practice squad. I guess I have to wait until someone fouls out before I can suit up again." I said flirtatiously. Sterling ignored what I said. He was standing so close to me wearing that seductive cologne. I had flashbacks of the night I met him, and he stood this close to me. He knew that turned me on, why was he trying to seduce me?

"Sheridyn, you used to take care of me when I was drunk." He repeated.

"Not my job anymore, it looks like someone else is the most valuable player." I said as I glanced over at Jessica. The crew stood around to have a firsthand glimpse at the harmony between us. Sterling stepped even closer staring into my eyes, seducing me with every word.

"So how are you doing, are you going to take care of me?"

"Well seems like you are in good hands already." I replied, looking towards Jessica again. No one could hear our dialogue, but I am positive they knew what was going on. Without so much as a gesture to the crowd, Sterling grabbed me by the hand and led me away from the crowd and outside the club to his truck.

"I don't want to interrupt your night. Jessica told me she had reservations with you, I don't want to steal her solo. I will need you to send my agent some game footage just in case I get traded." I said sarcastically. Sterling never bothered dignifying my comment with a response.

"We are going to Big Al's and hang out." Sterling said. I couldn't hold it in anymore.

"Jessica thought she was going home with you tonight, so you better not disappoint her. I need to know if her sex was as good as mine, are ya'll together or what?"

"Sheridyn, nobody's sex is as good as yours and no."

"Ok, then I need to understand why you are sleeping with her when you know I am always willing to give you some ass?

"I had sex with her twice before me and you started kicking it hard. If I knew you guys knew each other, I would have quit talking to her all together. We did it twice within a week or so. I haven't spent time with her since. We run in the same circles. It sort of just happened, her girl was kicking it with my boy and that's all it was." I just looked at Sterling as he continued.

"Every now and then, you gotta take a hit for the team. Sometimes, you just need a shot and sometimes, you want to get drunk." He exclaimed. Puzzled I replied,

"Ok you lost me."

"A shot of ass is just a little something to take the edge off. I have too much respect for you to do you like that.

In real life, I haven't even talked to her since you and I started kicking it. She didn't start calling me trying to hook up again until she found out about you." He explained.

"Are you telling me you will sleep with anyone that is willing to give you some? I understand your analogy but you get drunk on Crown so it makes since to do shots of Crown. But why are you taking Night Train shots?"

"It's not like that. Jessica and I know a lot of the same people, like I said; it was just kind of one of those things that happened." We never made it to Big Al's; we sat in his truck outside the club talking.

"Sheridyn, did you know that Greta's is up for sale?"

"Yeah, I heard that."

"Well me and some of my people are looking to buy it. That would be a cool moneymaker."

"Good luck, I am happy for you, I know ya'll will do well."

"Hell, they should give it to me as much money I spend there." This conversation was just a distraction; the Jessica issue was not resolved. I know I didn't have a right to try to regulate him, but I didn't like knowing he was seeing someone else at all.

Sterling leaned in to kiss me. I played hard to get by turning my head away from him because I was still bothered by the fact that he and Jessica had a thing. He rubbed his head along the side of my face.

"I miss you girl." Sterling whispered.

I couldn't resist him any longer; I gave in and kissed him. Our embrace was sensual. He rubbed his hands all over my body as we kissed. He tried to slide his hand under my dress between my legs.

"Let me in" he said softly. I grabbed his hand and moved it away.

"Baby, you can't touch it, I am on my cycle so you can't have treats tonight." I said.

"That don't matter to me Sheridyn, I want you to stay with me tonight. I want you, not your ass."

"Well I can't go with you right now; all my stuff is in Jessica's car."

"What stuff?"

"My purse, coat, and keys."

"Didn't your momma tell you never leave your purse anywhere?"

"I know, but I wasn't planning on being with you tonight, after all, you were supposed to be with Jessica, I just so happen to suit up tonight."

"I am taking you back to Greta's so you can get your stuff. You are coming to my house." He was being so firm, it was definitely a turn on. Were we about to enter negotiations on being a couple? I thought.

I hadn't realized it, but Sterling and I had disappeared for about an hour. Returning to Greta's, he didn't come inside, but insisted I get my things and come directly to his house. When I walked inside the club, I found Jessica and the other girls huddled together. I already know I was the topic of discussion because I was the only panther amongst all them cheetahs. I pretended like nothing had happened. The DJ announced that it was time to go. We headed to Jessica's car in silence.

"Damn it!" Jessica yelled.

"Oh my God what happened?" Jessica had smashed her finger closing the trunk. After making sure a trip to the emergency room wasn't necessary, we started on our way.

My cell phone rang. It was Sterling. I didn't answer the phone because I wanted to be respectful of Jessica's feelings and not rub my relationship with Sterling in her face. The atmosphere was already a little tense. He called back again, this time I decided to answer it.

"So where are you?"

"I am headed home."

"Home! I hope that you are just going home to get your car? Because Sheridyn in real life, I want you here. Do I need to come and get you?" Sterling asked.

"No, Jessica is dropping me off so I will call you later." I spoke as softly as possible, but I am sure Jessica knew what was going on but she was too afraid to ask questions. Another 5 minutes had passed, Sterling called again,

"Where are you? You should be on your way here by now."

"I haven't made it home yet."

"Dude, I put that on everything, I want you here."

"Ok, I will call you when I am on my way." After Jessica dropped me off, I got in my car and immediately headed to Sterling's place. I called him once I got in my car; he talked to me the entire time I drove.

I arrived at Sterling's apartment; he met me at the door with a tight hug and a big kiss. I took my heels off and left them at the door as we headed for the bedroom. I asked him for a t-shirt to wear so that I could get out of my "club" dress that reeked of smoke. This would be the first time I ever laid in bed with Sterling with clothes on. We cuddled close and Sterling kissed me on top of my head.

Lying on Sterling's chest, he started flipping through the television channels stopping on a movie. The romantic setting immediately disappeared when Sterling said,

"Oh my God, you have to watch this movie. It is funny as hell." We repositioned ourselves in the bed so that we could see the television. We watched the movie and laughed together. We both caught all the funny parts that probably no one else would have noticed. That is one of the things that I loved about him, we seemed to always be on one accord. I appreciated his sense of humor.

After the movie went off, we began to kiss. We were well into foreplay.

"Sterling, did you forget I am on my cycle?"

"I know I miss you and I want you so bad." There was no way I could bring him this far up the mountain to drop him. I kissed him intensely as I aggressively stroked him until he came in my hand. He squeezed me tightly and passed out. I looked at him and chuckled as he laid there so peaceful. I kissed him on his chest and tried to get up and go to the bathroom. He quickly woke up,

"Don't leave; I want you to stay here tonight." I assured him I was going to wash my hands. When I came back from the bathroom, I lied down beside him, he held me all night as we slept. The next morning, we were wakened by his sister coming to visit. This was my first time meeting her; this was not how I wanted to be introduced to anyone in Sterling's life. I was so embarrassed; I barely established eye contact when Sterling introduced us.

I didn't hear from Jessica all weekend, but I know she was waiting for me to arrive at the office on Monday. No soon as I logged onto my computer, Jessica appeared at my desk.

"Girl, look at my finger, I can't believe Sterling acted like that." Talk about a run on statement. Once again, avoiding the Sterling subject I said,

"Your finger looks pretty bad, but at least the swelling went down. Are you sure you don't need to go have a doctor look at that?"

"Sheridyn, I can't believe that Sterling acted the way he did on Friday, he is trying to play us." I was very puzzled so I asked,

"Is Sterling supposed to be your man or something?"

"Naw, but still you don't do stuff like that." I had no idea what she meant by that. What had this man done wrong?

"Jessica, I enjoy hanging out with you and more importantly, we have to work together. I cannot and will not discuss Sterling with you. I mean it." Puzzled she replied,

"Why? What's up with ya'll? By the way, you never told me how you know him."

"Jessica, none of that matters. I will not discuss him with you period. Again, thanks for inviting me to the party, I really enjoyed myself." Jessica gave a fake half assed smile and walked away. I knew she wasn't ready to hear the truth so I wasn't going to tell her the truth.

I was ready to start dating Sterling exclusively. All the events prior to this point indicated to me that the feeling might have been mutual, but I was not going to be the first to say anything about it, but I didn't want to mess things up either. We agreed that we weren't looking for a relationship when we first met and I know that if I brought it up, he would surely run in the opposite direction. But the more time I spent with him, the deeper my feelings became. I hate to admit it, but I was caught up. I was in love.

I am usually on top of my game, but this time, I had no idea what to do. I never felt like this about anyone before and I was scared of what I was feeling, I was scared of messing things up with him. I wish I had someone that could give me advice on how to play my cards. Sterling was the only man that I thought about marrying. I didn't know what to do.

Chapter VII

Madison, one of my friends from the office finally had her baby, after being out of commission for the past few months, she wanted to step out for just a brief moment for a quick drink and see if she could still toot it up. Greta's was a place to be if you were in a suit or if you were just casually cute. This was my first time hanging out with Madison because she found out that she was pregnant shortly after I went to work in her department. She was relocating back to Connecticut. I guess you could call this her going away celebration.

Madison often beat herself up because of everything she had been through and to make matters worse she was now a size 18. Although she was a shapely 18, was dark skinned, had mad sex appeal, pretty, and had a great personality, she didn't believe she could still turn heads. I decided to take her out so she could see that she still had it going on.

"Girl, I need to wind it up a couple of times before I leave the Mile High. I might get drunk from smelling liquor; you know I haven't had a drink in a year." Madison said.

"I guess I will have to be the designated driver because you need to make up for not getting your party on for a year." I responded. I drove past Greta's into the adjacent parking lot, I pointed because I saw Sterling. Madison had never met him, but I talked about him all the time to her.

"That's Sterling; look ain't he sexy as hell." I said with excitement.

"You are talking about that guy that is all in that girl's face."

"Yes ma'am, you can get drunk and I'm gonna get laid."

"Em" Madison replied with a condescending gesture. As if to say you are in love with someone that is in somebody else's face when you are not around. So far, Madison was not nearly impressed with Sterling as I was.

I wasn't concerned about the lady Sterling was talking to. They weren't standing close enough to be having an intimate conversation. We parked the car and walked towards the entrance of Greta's. Sterling noticed me, he immediately turned away from the lady he was talking to and greeted me with the biggest smile and a tight hug. He hugged me so tight that he lifted me off the ground.

"Baby, how you doing?" I was melting inside. I just loved the way he towered over me, held me and spoke.

"I am damn good."

"You sure in the hell are."

"I am sorry to interrupt your conversation, this is my friend Madison." He nodded at Madison never releasing me from his arms.

"It's nice to meet you Madison? Naw you aren't interrupting me." Sterling finally put me down and escorted us inside the club.

"What are ya'll sipping on? Drinks are on me." After paying for our drinks, Sterling excused himself to join his friends at the other side of the bar.

"Ok Sheridyn what was that all about? I mean that man loves you. His face lit up the whole street and the world disappeared when he saw you. He dismissed that girl with the quickness. It was like she was never there. Damn girl, explain to me why ya'll aren't together? He is so handsome to me and ya'll look so good together. Watching ya'll was like watching a scene from a movie."

With a baffled look I said,

"Girl, I have a better chance of discovering the cure for cancer than telling you why Sterling and I aren't a couple." Madison shook her head in disbelief as she sipped her drink.

"Have you told him how you feel about him?"

"Nope, he hasn't asked me to be his girl. When I first met him he said he didn't want a girlfriend and I don't want to rock the boat. I have a place in his life and that will have to do until I get a place in his heart."

"That's cute, but girl, you better tip that damn boat over, that is who you need to be with. Anybody can see that ya'll are in love. Somebody has to make the first move. Quit being a punk!"

Sterling and I casually flirted with each other all night. He frequently came over to check on me and Madison. Sterling noticed my drink was getting watery.

"Oh, you babysitting tonight? What's wrong with your drinker?"

"Sterling, I am not trying to get partly cloudy, and then go home by myself."

"I'll send you over another drink because you ain't gotta go home alone." He said before he walked away. I enjoyed just watching Sterling. Every time I heard his voice, saw him, or thought about him, I smiled. I enjoyed just being in his presence. Madison danced with Sterling's friend Jermaine a couple times, but for the most part, we all just hung out around the bar and chilled.

"You love the hell out that man don't you?" Madison said forcefully.

"Yes I do, but I enjoy just hanging out with him." Madison shook her head,

"I don't understand you at all, girl you better snatch that man up. If he don't know that you are in love with him, then how do you expect him to move on it?" I shrugged my shoulders. I had no idea why I was so weak for Sterling. I think I had to pretend that I was cool because of the scenario that was present when we first met each other. I had to show him that I knew how to keep my feelings under wraps.

Sterling and I never ran in the same circles but lately, we seemed to run into each other everywhere we went. Rize was this new spot that opened. Racine was my club buddy. I can't even remember how we became friends, but we complimented each other, and she was cool to kick it with. When Racine and I got to the club, we did our walk about. We walked through the entire club before buying a drink or dancing so we can check the scenery. We did this to scout out potential boos and to know what corners to stay away from.

Racine nudged me.

"That gots to be Sterling over there?" I looked up to see him at the bar passing a drink to Jermaine and smiling at me. His eyes were dancing, and his face was bright.

"Girl that boys face looks like Christmas. Yeah, he is definitely a Sheridyn boo. I see what Madison meant." I smiled and continued to walk towards him. As we approached the bar, Sterling greeted me with a hug and kiss. We joined him and his party. I introduced Racine to everyone as Sterling ordered our drinks. This was my first time seeing Max since I met him in Winter Park.

"Girl, how have you been? And where is your crazy ass friend? That girl was a space cadet." Max said as he gave me a tight hug.

"Everything is cool; I haven't talked to Sabrina since the last time I saw you."

"So what's up? When are we going to have that barbeque?"

"Hey you let me know. Come on let's go dance." Sterling stood back with a smile.

The DJ was rocking the place. The music was on hit. Sterling was watching so you know a sista was out there showing off, dropping it like it was hot. After just one dance Max said,

"I quit, you are too much for me. He escorted me back to the group.

"Man, girl got it going on, I can't hang." Sterling licked his lips and said,

"Sheridyn, can I hang?"

"I don't know, can you hang?"

"Sheridyn, I can hang right?"

"Are you going to play or pass?"

"Oh, I'm going to play." Max looked at us as we exchanged dialogue; I guess he didn't know Sterling and I hooked up after the Jazz Fest. We all started talking about the Jazz Fest and laughed as if it was just yesterday.

The fellas started complimenting me on how good I looked and you know they were checking out a sista's booty. Sterling made it known that we were kicking it by keeping me close to him so no one could see the booty. Racine and I were huddled up with the fellas. Periodically, I felt Sterling rubbing himself across my butt. He leaned in and whispered in my ear whenever he had something to say. I enjoyed the attention that he was giving me. The foreplay was worth the price of admission.

"Girl, let's go to the bathroom." Racine said.

"Ok." I looked at the fellas and said,

"We'll be back." I began to walk away, Sterling held onto my arm. I looked over my shoulder and smiled. He winked and released me.

"Ok, I'm not trying to be a hater or anything, but the fool got you on lock. So what's up with ya'll?" Racine asked the moment we were out of earshot.

"Girl, I can't call it. I just had this same conversation with Madison awhile ago. It is what it is."

"Well, what's up with the homeboys?"

"It depends on what you are looking for. I don't think any of them are boo material, but if you are just looking to kick it, then any one of them is an option." Racine and I found our own spot in the club away from Sterling and the fellas. We periodically checked in with them to share a few laughs and take pictures.

Sterling and I went to his place after the club. Sterling hit the bed and pretty much passed out. I had been drinking 1800 and flirting with him all night, I damn sure wasn't letting him go to sleep without giving me some first.

"Sterling come get in the shower." I insisted.

"Naw baby, let me lay here for a moment." That was man talk for *not tonight.* I wasn't having that. I started undressing him. He was a little irritated with me because I would not let him just lie there. He finally got up and stumbled to the shower. I hate drunk dick, but it was gonna have to do tonight because that 1800 had a sista on fire. My na na was screaming his name, she was not taking no for an answer.

Sterling leaned against the wall of the shower. He barely had his eyes opened. After noticing that the water had little effect on Sterling, I started nibbling on his back with little reaction from him. I grabbed the washcloth and made it very soapy. I washed Sterling down low and simultaneously nibbled on his nipples. That did the trick; Sterling grabbed both sides of my face and began to kiss me passionately underneath the stream of the water. He soaked my hair and kissed me as the water continued running down my face. We began to cover each other in soap; the suds fueled the inferno. We continued kissing and rubbing each other as we rinsed each other off.

Before I could get out the shower all the way and dry off, Sterling had laid on the bed with the towel draped across him and passed out again.

The shower or the foreplay didn't seem to faze Sterling at all, it was clear that the liquor had him, I was not gonna let this ride. I did what any woman in my position would do; I pulled out the big guns. I sat on top of him and started kissing his neck and his chest with little response from Sterling. Then I skipped to his feet. I started massaging his feet. I started licking and sucking on his toes. Sterling sat straight up in the bed as I fluttered my tongue across the bottom of his toes. I continued up his leg, biting his inner thigh scarcely licking across his genitals, I began to deep throat, taking all of him in my mouth. He quickly snatched me up and pulled my onto his face.

"Ride my tongue. I want you to cum all over my face." I didn't expect this. I had to make a mental note of this move. I positioned my body over his face and he squeezed my ass while he smothered his face deep inside my thighs. Once he knew I reached my peak, he rolled me onto my back.

We began having unbridled passionate sex that seemed to never end. We made love in a way that would make a porno star envious. Now I know what to do when I want daddy to act right. Suck the toes! We made love with so much zeal. I don't even remember our climatic conclusion; I just remember waking up in the wee hours of the morning to find no sheets, blankets, or pillows on the bed. Sterling and I were intertwined. Without waking him, I reached onto the floor and grabbed the comforter and pulled it over my head and covered us up.

I was falling deeper and deeper in love with Sterling, but what could I do? What should I say? I knew he had strong feelings for me, but he still hadn't mentioned a commitment yet. We spent time together and had a good vibe. We laughed and talked about everything. Not to mention the sex was off the hook. I did not understand the hang up.

One night after making love, we laid in bed and Sterling started talking,

"You know men are such simple creatures, we laugh at stuff that ain't even funny. We will laugh because something stinks. We will smell something laugh and say dude come smell this shit, man it stinks your boy laughs, and we will make jokes about it. That is something a man does. It's because of women we try to add a little depth to who we are." Was this my queue to ask him about us? What was he trying to say? Yes, I was a punk I just listened.

I decided this would be a good time to see where his head was.

"What do you think about marriage?" I asked casually.

"Marriage is cool, when I get married, I would just have a simple wedding with a family and a few close friends then go away for an extravagant reception. I want a honeymoon for something like two weeks on an island somewhere, and then come home to our new house. Weddings are a waste of money; it's something so that somebody somewhere can get some loot. See everyone that knows you before you get married should already know how much you love each other and the ceremony; it's just confirmation, a formality. I would rather be under the sun on a beach, making love and drinking for 2 weeks straight." You guessed it, I didn't say a word. I know I'm a punk.

I normally waited a day or two to call Sterling after I spent the night with him. I called him as little as possible to maintain his desire for me. I also didn't want him to think I was as sprung, but this time, he was on my mind, so I called the next day.

"Hello, are you busy?"

"Sheridyn, man Derrick had a heart attack. I just came home to change clothes, and then I am headed back to the hospital when my sister gets here. They are going to do open heart surgery on him."

"I am so sorry to hear that. What do you need for me to do?"

"Sheridyn, what can you do?" I knew he was frustrated, so I didn't take his words personal.

"I can pray for him, and I will come get that mountain of dirty clothes that is in your room. Laundry is one less thing you have to worry about."

"Damn baby, good looking out that would be cool as hell." I immediately left my house to go pick up the clothes. We packed up everything into my truck. I wanted to ask if he wanted me to go sit at the hospital with him, but I didn't.

"Call and let me know when Derrick gets out of surgery" came out instead. I kissed Sterling and left.

I took his clothes to a laundry mat, that way I could get it done quicker than washing them at home. I started sorting his clothes; I promise he was a true bachelor. Why was all his underwear raggedy? I wondered where did his nuts rest? Some of his underwear was ripped along the waistband like homemade jock straps. I am willing to bet Sterling only got new underwear when his mother bought them for him at Christmas. I just shook my head and threw all of them in the trash. While the clothes were washing at the laundry mat, I dashed to the store to buy him a couple packages of underwear, socks, and t-shirts. To replace the ones, I had thrown out. After his clothes were done being washed and dried, I folded them and packed them up, with his new socks and underwear.

Leaving the laundry mat, I noticed an adult bookstore. I remembered a conversation that Sterling and I had awhile ago about porno films. I decided I would surprise him with a movie. I thought he needed a little something to brighten his day.

I never knew there was more to buying a porno movie than just picking up one. There were rows and shelves full of movies. There were a couple of men browsing the shelves. After wandering aimlessly through the aisles for a while, I finally interrupted a gentleman browsing the section.

"Excuse me sir, what should I buy? Is there a bestseller or new release section?" I asked. The gentleman laughed.

"You must be shopping for your man."

"Yes. He is going through a little something. I wanted to give him a movie that would make him smile now and appreciate later." This man must frequent this store quite a bit because he broke it down for me,

"These have story lines and those over there are just sex."

"Ok what does that mean? Don't they all have sex in them?" I asked. The puzzled look on my face made the stranger chuckle. He proceeded to explain.

"Ok, do you want one that has acting in it or just have sex?" I shrugged my shoulders. I had never watched a porno; I threw it back on him.

"What do men like?" I guess he saw that the conversation was going nowhere fast so he grabbed two for me and said,

"Ok this one is good and this one is good."

"Most women aren't this open minded, you are a good woman." The stranger added. I thanked him as I read the back of the movie cases. I couldn't see the harm in watching a porno with Sterling, watching it meant we could experiment.

Sterling and I might learn something new. I am willing to try almost anything once. My thought was, we can try it, if we don't like it, we just won't do it again or we try it and like it, we have discovered a new way to please each other. Either way, I was in a win-win situation.

"Thanks again," I smiled and walked towards the cashier. I was excited to hear what Sterling thought of his new gift, but I decided to let him discover his big boy prize on his own instead of telling him that they were in the bag.

A couple of days had passed, and I had not heard from Sterling. They say no news is good news, but heart surgery is always risky business. I hesitated for a moment because I didn't want to come across as too pushy or overstepping my bounds. I decided to call anyway.

"Hey you, how is Derrick doing?"

"He made it through surgery, he is already asking for something to eat."

"Thank God, I am glad to hear that. Would you like your clothes back?"

"Sure, come on over." I called Sterling from the car to unload his clothes. Once we got inside, he didn't invite me to stay, I took that as my cue that he didn't want me to stay. I told Sterling that I would check on him later. He hugged me and gave me a quick peck on the lips. That let me know I had made the right decision by leaving. Much to my surprise later that evening, Sterling called.

"Sheridyn thank you so much for washing my clothes and picking me up some new underwear, although I could have used them drawls for a few more months."

"Stop it, your underwear was a thread away from being a jock strap."

"There wasn't nothing wrong with my underwear. Thanks for the special little gifts. Why didn't you stay and tell me that I had a lil something extra in the bag?"

"Well, I know you got a lot going on and I understand there are times a man needs "me time." I recognized today as one of those days. We have plenty of time to spend together in the future and reenact, I mean watch your new movies."

"Thanks so much, good looking out baby. I will wait until you come over so we can watch my new movies together." I know I scored some cool points with that, but it's been a couple years now and there was no change, he still hasn't said we were exclusive, and I definitely wasn't going to ask. At this point, he was the only man that I was sexually active with. I periodically dated, but nothing too serious because I didn't want to be in a relationship, just in case Sterling wanted to be exclusive.

Shockingly, Sterling called the next day.

"Baby, whatcha doing? You wanna cum. I'm sorry about that. I meant to say can you come over." I chuckled and responded,

"Let's cum together tonight, damn I meant to say, I would love to cum, come over your house tonight. Shall I bring anything?"

"Naw, you don't need nothing, somebody bought me this new flick yesterday that I thought we should watch together."

"Really? Someone must like you a lot. I'll leave here at 10 after I get the kids in bed."
Sterling met me at the door with a passionate kiss and we went directly into his bedroom.

"Baby, open the movie and stick it in the VCR while I go get us some wine." I opened and loaded the movie while Sterling was in the kitchen. When he returned, we assumed our positions in bed to watch the movie like it was a new release. We toasted and sipped the wine, the movie started. Sterling and I didn't need any outside stimulants to get us started or keep our beat. The movie was not on for more than five minutes when Sterling started kissing me. We were undressed, enjoying our first orgasm before the couple on the screen could get undressed. I believe that was too much for both of us. We just passed out. We never turned off the movie.

Before I knew it, the sun was up. When I stayed out all night, I would always try to make it home before the kids woke up. I tried to get out of bed to get dressed, but I woke Sterling up. Without him opening his eyes, he pulled me on top of him to get a little something before starting his day and of course, I didn't mind waking up to a quickie either.

A couple weeks had passed, and I had not heard from Sterling so I called.

"Hey baby!"

"What's up girl?" Sterling sounded as though he was out of breath and scared.

"What's wrong? Is Derrick ok?"

"On my way home from work today I was almost killed. Sheridyn I am telling you it wasn't nothing but the grace of God that saved me. Baby for real, I really should be dead right now."

"What happened?"

"Man Sheridyn, damn. I should be dead right now." I saw this conversation was going nowhere fast.

"Sterling, I am on my way over, ok?"

"Sure come on over and I will tell you what happened." I threw on a jogging suit and headed to Sterling's apartment. Passing by a grocery store, I decided to stop and buy him a card and some flowers to cheer him up. There were slim pickings in the floral department at 10 o'clock at night, but I found something that didn't look too feminine. Arriving at Sterling's apartment, I found him in the kitchen cooking a grilled cheese sandwich. I think in all the time I had known him; this was my first time ever seeing him in the kitchen. He didn't greet me with affection when I came through the door. I presented him with the flowers and card.

He read the card, thanked me, positioned the glass vase on the kitchen table and gave me a cordial hug.

Sterling paced the floor back and forth and started telling me what had happened.

"Sweetheart, I was on I-25 when this 18-wheeler came flying from an on ramp at a 100 miles per hour headed straight towards me. I didn't know what to do. I couldn't speed up or slow down to avoid him hitting me. I closed my eyes and yelled Jesus. Somehow, the truck missed me. I promise you it was nothing but God. That truck should have slammed right into me." Sterling continued pacing the floor, consistently flipping his grilled cheese with the spatula and opening the refrigerator. I sat and listened attentively as he kept repeating the story out loud.

I knew there was nothing I could say that would comfort him or identify with what he was feeling; I needed to calm him down.

"Baby, come take a shower and relax." I suggested.

"Naw I'm cool." Sterling continued to pace the floor and vigorously flip his grilled cheese that was more than well done. I stood up, turned off the stove, grabbed him by the hand and said,

"Come take a shower now." Reluctantly, he followed me through his bedroom to his bathroom. I turned the water on and started undressing him. While he was in the shower, I straightened up his room. He was a bachelor not expecting company and his room reflected just that. There were clothes that he had worn to the office draped across a chair, gym shoes, and an assortment of dirty clothes scattered across the floor.

After about 10 minutes, I heard the water stop. I met Sterling in the bathroom with a towel.

"Don't dry off, come with me." I grabbed his towel and laid it across the bed.

"Lie down on your stomach." I used another towel to dry him off. While he was in the shower, I turned on the stereo and lit some candles. I started at his feet, massaging him with lotion.

"Sterling just relax, clear your mind, and let me do this." This moment was all about him. I massaged his body attentively and worked the lotion into his muscles. Other than the soft music from his stereo, the room was still and quiet.

As I moved up his legs and began to rub his back, Sterling turned around looked at me and said,

"I was with a woman for seven years and she never made me feel like I do right now." He turned back onto his stomach. I just sighed as the tears began to swell in my eyes. I wanted to tell him that the reason I made him feel this way was because he was feeling my love. After his near-death experience, I didn't want to lose him without him knowing how I really felt about him, but I was more scared of losing him because I told him how I felt inside and being rejected. I was told you are never supposed to tell a man that you love him unless they say it first and besides, we never had "the talk." The, *what do we mean to each other and how are we going to classify our relationship talk."*

I continued to rub his muscles and the more he relaxed, the harder my heart pounded. I searched within myself to find the courage and the words to tell him that I loved him, but the circuits between my mouth, heart, and mind were not functioning together. I opened my mouth, but the words didn't come out.

Since I couldn't bring myself to tell Sterling that I loved him, I decided that I would show him, I thought. I signaled Sterling to turn on his back to massage and lotion the front of his body. I straddled myself across his thighs. I rubbed the lotion in my hands across his chest up towards his neck and Sterling grabbed me by both of my wrists, pulled me to him, and began to kiss me. He let my hands go only to begin to passionately run his fingers through my hair and kiss me harder. In one quick motion, he turned me onto my back and started undressing me. He kissed my body with each time piece of clothing he removed.

Now that I was undressed, he sat up on his knees looking down at me. I sat up to kiss him. He pushed me down to the bed and spread my legs apart. He started kissing me deep inside. With nothing but my clit between his lips, he gently fondled me with his tongue. Oh, God the feeling was so intense that I began to squirm and breathe deeply. He wrapped his arms over my quivering thighs locking his hands at my waist. There was no way I could move.

"Just let it go baby, cum for me, cum for me now." He whispered in a stern voice. I was trying to hold it but I began to explode from within.

"That is what I wanted, let it go. Give it to me." He said tenderly as he lessened the intensity of his caress.

Once the shivering in my legs ceased, He let my legs go as he slid himself inside of me. We began to make love more powerful and passionately than we had ever done in the past. I was left breathless; the rhythm was intense. All I could utter were the sweet sounds of ecstasy and sheer pleasure. I threw my leg over Sterling's head and turned over onto my stomach while holding him inside of me. Now that we were in position, I got on my knees, arched by back so that my ass was tooted high up in the air. Sterling started right in, stroking it just the way I liked it.

We always made harmonious love. We were always in sync. As Sterling approached his climatic point, he began to move deeper; he reached out for my hair, reaching underneath my arm to grab my hair on the top of my head.

"Damn girl, shit Sheridyn." The bed collapsed underneath us. Somehow, we managed to break the bed. It didn't matter to us; we laughed and kept it moving.

I turned back over and rolled Sterling on his back so that I would be on top of him. I began to ride him. As Sterling caressed my body and lightly smacked my ass, the sound of sex echoed through the room. I leaned forward and whispered,

"Is daddy ready to cum?"

"Yes" he whimpered. In a sweet, sexy, alluring voice, I asked again,

"Is daddy ready to cum? Are you ready to cum for me daddy?" He screamed,

"Yes! I'm about to cum." I felt his body tense up, I immediately jumped off him and began to suck his erection vigorously. The freak in me came out, Sterling pushed down on my shoulders to signal that he was starting to cum, I began sucking him harder. I swallowed him completely. Sterling screamed with a high-pitched voice and struggled to push me off him, but I had him tightly gripped between the roof of my mouth and my tongue. His entire body quivered.

When Sterling finished cumming and there was nothing left, I loosened the grip my mouth had on him and licked my tongue across his tip. He pulled me onto his chest and held me there tightly. I felt the aftershocks shoot through his body. I could barely breathe because Sterling had me clinched so tightly into his chest. He held me until he fell asleep. I pretty much knew it was a wrap after that; I was surely kicked off the team.

Over the next couple of weeks, I periodically called Sterling, but he never returned my calls. Just as I suspected, either he longer respected me for my performance in bed, or I blew his mind. Nevertheless, it felt like I had lost my best friend, not my lover. I am glad I didn't tell him that I loved him; at least I can save face. It hurts a little and I miss him like crazy, but it's all good. I wish I could just lie in his arms. Not knowing what was up caused my imagination to run wild. The "I wonder why" game is a bitch.

Chapter VIII

I decided to stop by the Goal Post for a quick drink. The Goal Post was a neighborhood bar where the blue collar workers stopped before they headed home. I liked to go there because my Aunt Gwen ran the kitchen there. I walked into the Goal Post where Pete greeted me. I affectionately called him Uncle Pete. Even when Sterling was nowhere to be found, Pete would always make sure I was well taken care of. As you can imagine, he played the role of pussy police. Pete made sure there was no chance another brotha was going to holla at me if he was in the vicinity. I had to ask Pete,

"Uncle Pete what's up with your boy? I promise I love that man and I want to be his one and only, but he doesn't seem interested. I know he cares about me, but why the cold shoulder all of a sudden?"

"Sheridyn, Sterling knew after the first time ya'll slept together, you were more than just a bootie call." Puzzled I replied,

"Ok, what in the hell does that mean?"

"Sheridyn, he wasn't prepared for what he got when he hooked up with you. You are going to have to stop sleeping with him so that he can get to know you outside the bedroom."

"Uncle Pete, how am I supposed to do that, you know good and hell well that we have an insatiable appetite for each other."

"I'm telling you, stop sleeping with him."

The fact that I was having this conversation with Pete was off the wall to begin with. Pete was a Q-Dawg, a *Bruh fo' life.* Commitment isn't in the by laws of the Bruhs, but as Pete spoke, I saw honesty and sincerity in him.

"Baby girl, don't give up on him. He does love you."

"Pete, I gave Sterling all that I had in me. But it seems like the more I give, the more he runs in the opposite direction. I know he loves me but when are we gonna get together for real."

"Baby girl, I'm a man and I'm telling you, quit sleeping with him and let him see what kind of woman you are outside the bedroom. He knows you are a good girl, but he doesn't know what type of a woman you are. A man needs to know that you can take care of the house and kids. He has to know he can leave his wallet around and be confident you won't steal his money or rummage through it. Trust me. Although men want a woman that is uninhibited in the bedroom and stick her sore toe in a pot of red beans and rice, the more you toot it up, the harder it is for him to see that you are that woman, capable of fulfilling both needs."

Pete's advice seemed wise and simple enough to follow. I smiled inside because Pete let me know I had at least been the topic of conversation at some point.

"Baby girl, I am outta here, are you all right?"

"I am good, thanks for the advice."

I called Sterling to invite him on dates and he consistently declined. Sterling had never been to my house or met my children so I invited him to dinner. I even asked if he would come cut the boys hair, he declined that as well. How could I follow Pete's advice if Sterling wouldn't let me? Did I scare him away? Did someone else grab his attention? What the hell?

I felt a little empty not having Sterling in my life. I dated around a little, but no one looked at me the way Sterling did. No one found the same things funny; let's face it, I wanted Sterling no one else would measure up. I missed the intellectual conversations that we shared. I missed laughing with him. I even missed his touch. I had to figure out what I was doing wrong because I was not ready to live my life without him.

I went to my mother's beauty shop to get my hair done; Ms. Shirley just so happened to be there as well. Ms. Shirley was an older lady that frequented my mother's beauty shop. She possessed great insight and gave good advice when it came to men. You would never guess that she would talk so openly and candidly, but she shot straight from the hip without the "well back in my day" tone.

"Ms. Shirley, I am head over heels for this man." I said.

"Baby, tell me about him." I went through the whole spiel of how much in love we were and how I knew he was perfect for me. Ms. Shirley listened attentively. When I finally finished my dissertation, she grabbed my hands and said,

"I can see you love that man but let me tell you something. You are just convenient for him. He doesn't love you; he just loves the fact that you love him." Ms. Shirley noticed the expression on my face was not very receptive.

"I am not trying to hurt your feelings, but it didn't matter who was there during those touching moments, he just needed someone. As far as he is concerned, you could have been one of the boys from the basketball court. Let me explain it to you this way. He reached out and grabbed you; he didn't reach out to you. There is a difference. He never called you when something was wrong; it was just a coincidence that you called him. Better yet, has he called you to check on you? Has he followed up with you after a bad day? Or brought you soup when you were sick? He is only concerned about his own needs. You are supposed to complete him, and he is supposed to pour into you. Is that happening?"

This time, Ms. Shirley was off. She usually gave sound advice, but I am certain she didn't understand what I was talking about.

"Remember one thing Sheridyn, a man will only allow himself to get hurt one time, which means if he is unwilling to hurt, he is equally unwilling to love." I heard what Ms. Shirley said, but she didn't hear what I said. She would have had a different opinion if she had only saw us together because I know what Sterling and I shared was deeper than just the convenience of a booty call.

"Tell me Sheridyn, what do the kids think about him?"

"They've never met him. I don't let men meet my kids until I'm sure he is going to be in my life for awhile." I answered.

"Sheridyn, baby, honey as much as you are disagreeing with me, you already have the answer in your heart. First, you've not made your intentions known to him. Then, you have been seeing this man for a couple years, now you say you want to be with him, but you haven't found him worthy enough to meet your kids. I think you should reassess this relationship." I listened, but Ms. Shirley didn't understand the situation.

Later that same evening, I asked Twist what I should do, you know get a man's perspective. Twist was my platonic friend that I used to decipher man speak for me. He was a pro-football player that adopted me as his family. He married a piece of arm candy that couldn't cook, so he made it a point to dine at my house a couple days a week. And since he didn't have children, he loved tossing the football around with my boys. Once again, I gave the whole spiel to Twist, ending it with what should I do?

"Sheridyn I hate to bust your bubble, but he doesn't love you, in fact, he's hating on you."

"How could he possibly be hating on me?"

"As long as a man can make you think he loves you, he knows that you are committed to him. He can do whatever he wants, but you will sit tight and wait. And even better, he can dog you out, throw you a Scooby snack, you will forgive him and come running back."

I valued Twist's opinion, but what he was saying did not make sense to me at all. But I listened with hopes of gaining more understanding. Twist continued,

"Women often make up fictitious loving relationships, when in reality; your relationship is one of convenience. Since you are making me go there, I will call a spade a spade. You are just a booty call to him. No matter what he does, he knows you will be there. You will give him some ass and he doesn't have to work for it, pay for it, or even ask for it. Once again, you give him the convenience of a girlfriend without a commitment." No one understood what I shared with Sterling. I know Sterling thinks I am more than just a booty call. I had to really argue my point.

"If Sterling didn't love me, why does his face light up when he sees me?"

"Hell, a man's face will light up when the newest Madden game is released so don't be impressed. You know I love you right?"

"Right."

"How do you know that?"

"Because I can depend on you, you comfort me when I am having a bad day. You are a role model to the children; I can talk to you about anything."

"Ok, you know I love you because I show you, you assume Sterling loves you because he looks like it. Think about it. Would you rather deal with someone who shows you they love you or someone who looks like they love you?" Twist was on a role, he kept talking.

"Sheridyn, the best advice I can give you is, if you really love him, let him go because he is not ready. If you hold on, he will just continue to hurt you and when or if he is ready to settle down, he will be too busy trying to heal the hurts of the past rather than loving you." I know what I felt. Sterling is the only man I have ever considered marrying. We were so perfect together. But I refused to believe everyone else was right.

Every couple of weeks or so I would call Sterling with no response. I have never had this much trouble with a man or a relationship for that fact of the matter. I have walked away from men for less than what I am letting Sterling get away with. I needed to do some soul searching. I deserved better than what I have been allowing Sterling to give. I know in relationships you have to compromise, but I could not understand why I was settling. My mind played tricks on me. Was I not good enough for him? Why didn't he choose me? I guess I need to face the fact things between us were over.

As soon as I made up my mind that I was walking away from Sterling, he managed to pop back into my life and like a dumb ass, I welcomed him in with open arms and legs.

"Hey Sheridyn, what's up? It's Sterling."

"This is a pleasant surprise, how are you sir?" It has been a few months since I had talked to him.

"Remember my boy Drake that I was telling you about? You know the one that plays in the NBA? Well, Denver just picked him up so you know I gotta show my boy a good time. Can you call your girl Racine to kick it with him? Is she cool? I don't want to hook him up with some groupie bitch. Excuse my language."

"Yeah, that would be cool; Racine will kick it if he's cute. We ain't trying to go out with anyone that looks like a Cyclops."

"Holla at your girl and see if you can make that happen and get back at me. He will be here at the end of the week." I guess Sterling was telling the truth about having childhood friends in the NBA. This was the first time he brought him up since we first met. Sterling didn't say that he missed me, wanted to see me, or what I've been up to but at least he called.

Later that evening, I talked to Racine and she was down to kick it. She never passed up the opportunity to be wined and dined for free. I called Sterling and let him know that everything was all good. Although we set up a date, the initial meeting never happened. Once again, Sterling and I couldn't get our ducks in a row or even in the same pond long enough to hook up. Then to compound matters, Drake was traveling with the team and that limited our availability as well.

By happenstance, Racine and I ran into Sterling and Drake at the nightclub. I introduced Drake and Racine. Drake and Racine were mutually pleased with each other. I was dressed scantly clad. Sterling had never seen me dressed in nightclub attire and it didn't go over too well. While Racine and Drake were getting acquainted with one another, Sterling and I began to argue. For the life of me, I can't remember what we were arguing about, but something was definitely different between us.

Sterling ordered me to go home with him; I was even told to ride with him in Drake's car. I tried to get out of riding with them by telling him I drove.

"Racine and I will meet you guys at your place." I said with my keys in hand. Sterling was not having that. He demanded that Racine drive my car and I ride with him and Drake.

Sterling escorted me to Drake's Mercedes and directed me to sit inside while he and Drake continued to holla at their boys. Racine pulled up next to the passenger window where I was sitting. Since the guys weren't in the car, Racine called my cell laughing,

"So Sterling got you on lock! Damn girl what did you do?"

"I ain't done nothing. I think my outfit might be a little too bootylicious for him."

"His boy Drake is fine, I think I'm gonna have to holla at that there." Racine and I chatted until the crowd of men dispersed. Sterling and I argued all the way to his apartment. This was strange because we had never had an argument before.

We arrived at Sterling's apartment, he handed me one of his t-shirts and ordered me to put it on. The t-shirt was a

4x so it hung on me like a tent; however, it hid the booty. Racine arrived minutes later.

"Damn, daddy made you change quick as hell." Racine snickered under her breath as she walked through the door. Drake and Racine engaged in small talk between me and Sterling's squabbling. The inevitable happened, Racine and Drake headed to Sterling's room. I believe they were trying to get away from the arguing more than they were trying to get with each other. Sterling and I couldn't get our foreplay going because we were still bickering.

Things between Sterling and I finally started to wind down. We were about to get busy. I was straddling him in the chair, and we began to kiss. He nibbled on my ear and neck. I rubbed his chest and began to unfasten each other's clothes. Out of nowhere, we heard a loud smack. Drake must have smacked Racine's ass. Sterling and I busted out in simultaneous laughter.

"In real life, I know she has a handprint on her ass."

"Damn, Sterling is your boy that carried away? I guess we know who got the smack down for real."

"Whatever girl, my boy can handle his business."

"Should I try and find him a saddle?" We laughed as we laid back in the recliner and began to talk. This was the first time Sterling and I had ever been together and never took the opportunity to have sex.

Drake and Racine surfaced from the bedroom a couple hours later. Sterling and I couldn't help but laugh. Racine and Drake joined in the laughter. I know he thought he was going to get some, but I wasn't in the mood anymore. Besides, I had to take Racine home. I know that was just an excuse because Drake could have taken her home, but I was trying to follow Pete's advice.

Racine and I planned to hang out with Twist and the gang. Because we were running late, I drove instead of riding with the fellas. Upon pulling into the parking lot of Sadie's, we saw a black Benz with Florida plates. That meant Drake was in the house and Sterling was definitely close by. Racine and I didn't say a word; we just looked at each other, did our happy dance, and hummed a tune. We knew we were gonna get us some, and it was gonna be good. Nobody was going to have to take a hit for the team. We checked our makeup in the rearview mirror and scurried to the door. Before we got all the way inside the club good I ran into Clayton.

"Racine look there is Clayton."

"Who is he?"

"Girl, that's the guy that I was kicking it with until I called his job one night and they said he wasn't back from his honeymoon. Then, he had the gull to show up on my doorstep the day after he came from his honeymoon like nothing was wrong, trying to get some ass."

"So, he really thought you were Lucy Lunchmeat?"

"Yes, he told me he was a geographical bachelor, which means he's only married when he is in city limits. Watch, he is going to ask me what's up for tonight."

"Hey Sheridyn, what's going on girl?" Clayton said as he hugged me. I lingered in Clayton's arms as we exchanged small talk, or shall I say, as he presented his case on why I should let him do it to me. Racine stood beside me snickering with her head pointed forward. That was a context clue to let me know that Sterling was in sight and approaching. I let Clayton go just as Sterling approached us.

"Sterling this is Clayton, Clayton this is Sterling." They mugged each other for a moment then Sterling stepped in front of Clayton to greet me. Sterling gave me a deep, tight hug. I tingled all over. It had been a few weeks since we made love so the na na was jumping at the thought that we were gonna get some. I ignored Clayton so he got the hint and got ghost.

Racine and I followed behind Sterling as he led us to Drake where the waitress was standing by to take our drink order.

"Sheridyn, that was too funny. I am mad Clayton got a whole wife and he has the nerve to try to regulate you. And Sterling needs to quit playing, he know he loves you, ya'll need to go ahead and get married." Racine snickered.

"Girl, now that Drake is here, I know good and hell well that ain't gonna happen. With all the groupies that are chasing Drake, Sterling won't have no problem getting his share of ass too." I responded.

After taking a sip of my drink, Sterling grabbed my hand and led me to the dance floor. Sterling and I danced real close and seductive. The anticipation of what the evening would have in store heightened. The atmosphere was great. Sterling had the sexiest mouth. All I could think about was his mouth all over my body.

"Sheridyn, are you gonna ride my tongue tonight?"

"If I ride your tongue, it's only fair that I swallow." Sterling closed his eyes as he reminisced about how that would feel.

"We ain't talking about swallowing."

"Well, you swallow my juices when you lick on me, why can't I swallow your juice when I suck on you?" Sterling pulled me close and shook his head. As bad as I wanted him, Pete's words *stop sleeping with him* kept playing over and over again in my mind. I had to resist and not go home alone with him. I was already moist and being partly cloudy didn't help matters any. The only way I was able to escape was to disappear into the crowd and duck out while Sterling wasn't looking. Racine and I never met up with Twist. I love a good distraction.

Racine noticed one of her boos on the other side of the club and decided she was going to kick it with him for the night. That would be my out. When Racine and her male friend left, I slipped away as well. I guess this meant another lonely night for me. Clayton called later that night trying to hook up, but I never heard from Sterling just as I thought his attention was sidetracked by someone else. Oh well, such is life. I was disappointed but I trusted Pete and I was determined to follow his advice.

I had to find something to do to keep me from thinking about Sterling. Technically, I was just a booty call with benefits, and I let myself get caught up. I needed someone to divert my attention away from Sterling. The following week, I decided to go to Greta's by myself and meet me a new boo. There was absolutely nothing going on there, this was a first. There were only three people in the entire club. It had been a while since I had been to Club Ray's, it was a dive, but it was on the way back to my house. I pulled up at Club Ray's, the parking lot was packed, this would explain why Greta's was empty.

As luck would have it, as I walked into Club Ray's, the first person I saw was Pete with an ear to ear grin.

"Come here baby girl and hug my neck. You look good as pot liquor." Pete was as country as they came. Before I could get my arms around him to hug his neck Pete said,

"You know your boy is here and is happy to see you." Pete let me go; I turned around to see Sterling standing behind me. I smiled,

"How you doing?" I seductively asked.

"I am fucking great."

"Oh, I already know." Sterling hugged and kissed me.

"Baby you are behind and you gotta catch up." I was puzzled until I saw the waitress putting three shots of Goose and two shots of Hen on the table.

"Who else is with ya'll?" I asked.

"Nobody, the Hen is for me and Pete, the Goose is all on you."

"What? If I drink all 3 of them shots, I am bound to take advantage of you tonight?"

"What you scared?" Once again, I did what any woman in my position would do. I drank all 3 of my shots back-to-back, knowing those shots was gonna put me on my ass. But I had to prove that I could handle mine. Pride will get you caught up every time.

Everything seemed to be cool. The three of us laughed and talked. The DJ decided to throw in a slow set; Sterling invited me to dance. We moved close and seductively. Listening to Sterling breathing close to my ear sounded like a sweet melody.

"So what you gone do?" Sterling asked.

"What cha want me to do?" Why did I open that can of worms?

"I want you to scream my name." Sterling answered.

"Is that all daddy want? Because I can scream your name right now."

"I want to cum tonight like never before."

"I'll see what momma got up her sleeve for you tonight."

"I'm ready, are you ready? Is the kitty wet?"

"Na na is ready, wet, and able!"

"Pete rode with me though."

"I will give Pete my car and ride you, I mean ride with you."

"Let's do it." Sterling said as he led me off the dance floor.

We explained the game plan to Pete and he was cool with it. I was surprised that Pete didn't give me the "don't you do it look." We left Pete at the club by himself. Sterling and I got in his truck. I immediately started taking off my pants. I hung my g-string on his rear-view mirror. I grabbed Sterling's hand and put it between my legs.

"What you know about that?" He rubbed his fingers between my legs, then stuck his fingers in his mouth and sucked my juice off his fingertips and said,

"I know all about that." I began to unloose his pants and exposed his erection. Driving down the highway, I leaned over and began to suck his tip.

"Tell me what you know about that?" He said,

"I'm gonna show you what I know about that as soon as we get to the house."

We savagely pawed each other at every stop light until we made it to his house. After Sterling parked the truck, I climbed on top of him and began to ride him.

"Baby, you gotta stop, I can't hit it right like this. Let's take it inside." We walked to his door half dressed with my g-string still hanging from the rear view mirror. Once inside his house, never stopping long enough to turn on the lights, Sterling turned the stereo on as we hit the bed. We began to make love wildly, giggling and whispered like teenagers sneaking to have sex.

I made love to Sterling with no inhibitions. I wonder what he thought of me. I don't think he knew that he was the only person that had experienced this part of me. I even wondered why I felt comfortable enough to get so intimate with him and try things with him that I would have never considered doing with someone else. It must be love.

Over the next several months, I tried to see Sterling, but there was no haps. I was starting to think that if I wasn't sleeping with him, he didn't think there was a reason that we should see each other. I could never get him on the phone. If I left a message, he never returned my call. I guess it was over between us. But I still held on because he never said it was over.

I decided to pick up a part time job at a high-end department store so that I can get a discount on Christmas gifts for my friends and family. Much to my surprise, Sterling walked in with a girl. He barely looked in my direction when he spoke. Was this the girlfriend? Was she the reason that I hadn't heard from him in months? I wondered. They didn't look happy together, more importantly, he looked embarrassed that I saw them together. For the record, she wasn't even cute. My feelings were hurt, but there was not a lot that I could say. Sterling looked surprised to see me. I was a little jealous because we hadn't been on a date in over a year.

It was true that he had slipped and said he loved me a couple of times, but I think Twist was right when he said Sterling was just hating to keep me on lock while he did his thug-thizzle. I guess it was finally time to move on. I had quit calling Sterling all together and he hadn't bothered to call me either. Anything that was as good as what Sterling and I had together was not meant to last forever. We fulfill dreams, while fantasies are imaginary. Its time to face the fact that being with Sterling was a fantasy.

Several months had passed, I still thought about Sterling quite often. I began to wonder if Pete's advice was just a nice way of telling me that Sterling was only interested in having a sexual relationship with me. Ever since I stopped having sex with Sterling, he stopped being interested. I refused to believe that I was just a bootie call, but the signs were pointing in that direction.

Chapter IX

My little sister Brooklyn decided to move to Colorado. She was recently divorced, and she needed to get away from her overbearing ex- husband. I adored my sister. This was our first opportunity really hanging out as adults. Brooklyn had a quirky, girl next door look about her. She married right out of high school and was back on the dating scene after six years. Brooklyn was anxious to meet men and see what was really going on in Colorado.

I took Brooklyn to Greta's to get her feet wet. I thought this was the perfect club to remind her of home. We walked into the nightclub where people who had not seen me in awhile greeted me at the door. I noticed a woman staring at us from across the bar. I didn't know her but she looked at me then looked away. When she looked away, I noticed Sterling. She looked back and forth at the both of us.

After several meet and greets, I made it to the bar to order drinks for me and Brooklyn. I introduced Sterling to my sister; he gave me a casual hug and asked how my kids were doing. That was strange that he asked about the kids immediately. What made his behavior even stranger is that he didn't offer to buy me a drink and I didn't see his entourage of homeboys that normally accompanied him. Brooklyn and I left the bar and headed to the dance floor never seeing Sterling again. There was so much eye candy in Greta's that night truthfully, I forgot all about Sterling. Brooklyn had the time of her life. She wasn't sure if the club was all that or if it was because she was single again but whatever it was, it was fun.

Greta's became the spot for Brooklyn. I think it reminded her of the clubs back in Chicago. Greta's was one stop shopping. Everybody who was anybody was guaranteed to pass through sometime during the night. Greta's became a weekly stop for us. Twist and his boy Thomas joined us for drinks one night. Thomas was interested in Brooklyn. Although Twist and I were just friends, we thought about crossing that line a few times, but we always realized it would be more trouble than it was worth. If Brooklyn hooked up with Thomas, I would have been left hanging.

I began to see Sterling's entourage pile into Greta's. That meant my options were opening up, Sterling must be one his way, I thought. Sterling had a boy that was interested in Brooklyn too. All I needed was an excuse to get naked with Sterling. The whole crew was accounted for except Sterling. Derrick walked over to where Brooklyn and I were standing, he gave Twist dap and me a hug. When he hugged me he whispered,

"Does Sterling know you're here?"

"No, Sterling and I aren't seeing each other anymore so I don't check in with him." Derrick nodded. He pulled his cell phone out of his pocket and made a call as he walked away. Greta's wasn't really jumping at all.

"What's up, ya'll let's roll to Climaxx, that new spot downtown." Twist suggested.

"That's cool, let's finish these drinks first. We will just follow ya'll because I have never been there before." I turned away from Twist to pick up my drink when I noticed that same girl from a few weeks ago walk towards me. She looked directly in my face, turned around, and walked out the club. Ok, what was that all about? I wondered. I wasn't drinking anything else. I had to be on my *p's and q's* because I didn't know this woman or why she looks at me the way she does. Did she have beef with me or was she hating on my sister? I needed to be ready for whatever.

Somewhere in the midst of the crowd, Sterling emerged. He hugged me as he looked over my head. We exchanged pleasantries and he walked back to his crowd of friends. Sterling always assumed that Twist and I were kicking it. He didn't understand or believe that two attractive people of the opposite sex could have a platonic relationship. But what Sterling didn't know is I knew all of Twist's dirt and that was the reason why we were only friends. Sterling seemed a little distant. He didn't joke me, offer to buy a drink, ask for a dance or nothing. Was he really tripping that hard over me being with Twist?

Apparently, Sterling was on one today, but I wasn't going to trip with him, I was still heading to Climaxx with Twist and the crew. Thirty minutes had passed, and we were just about to walk out the door. Twist was more popular than I was. He had to talk to everybody that crossed his path. He even stopped for a quick shot with one of the other players on the team before we walked out the door. Finally, we made it to the parking lot. Brooklyn and I followed Twist and Thomas in my truck.

Walking inside of Climaxx as a foursome, I saw Sterling and his friend Ricky out of the corner of my eye walking in the club also. I pretended I didn't see them. I didn't have anything to hide, or anyone to answer to, but I know what it looked like. Things with Sterling and I were over and I needed to get over him. For what it was worth, I still cared about what he thought of me though.

As soon as I walked in the door, I saw Drew. I dated Drew many years ago. We met at a party. He played football when we were dating. He was a 6'6, 320lb, sexy tight end from DC. I thought we were exclusive until I found out he got this high school girl pregnant while we were dating. Needless to say, that killed the romance between us. This was my first-time seeing Drew in years. I guess I was a sight for sore eyes. He hugged me and held on for a moment. If I didn't know any better, I would have thought he missed a sista. Seconds after Drew let me go; he raised his arm up over my head to give someone behind me a pound. When I turned around to see who it was, much to my surprise, it was Sterling. He was surprised to see that I was the woman in Drew's arms. When Drew let me go, Sterling gave me a cordial hug. As I faced both of them, I said,

"It was great seeing you guys again." I immediately turned and dismissed myself.

The night progressed, Sterling's friend Ricky and Brooklyn were inseparable. I didn't know much about Ricky. I've seen him around, but this was my first time formally meeting him. But Brooklyn took to him. Twist ran into one of his scrumpets so that meant he was on lock. Sterling and I hadn't danced or talked all night but we were the designated drivers for the night. Something was destined to transpire. I was ready to go, Ricky, Sterling, Brooklyn, and I huddled together.

"So, what's the plan?" Sterling asked. I shrugged my shoulders. And no one else spoke up either.

"Ok, Ricky you ride with Brooklyn and Sheridyn you ride with me." Sterling insisted. Sarcasm was my middle name, so I interjected,

"That works, Sterling you can drop me off at home if it ain't a problem."

"Naw it's not a problem, but you ain't going home tonight. You are coming with me." He demanded.

"Are you cool?" I asked Brooklyn as I gave her my keys. She nodded with a smile. That let me know she was not disappointed about how the evening was unfolding.

Sterling and I didn't say anything to each other as we walked to the car. Sterling went in the opposite direction of where he lived. He pulled up at a hotel not too far from the club. I didn't ask why we were at a hotel. But Sterling went through a long drawn out story of why he was living in a hotel. I knew it was a bunch of bullshit, so I selectively listened to him. I am always doubtful when a person volunteers an explanation before a question is asked. When we walked inside the hotel room, his room looked like he had been there for a few days and that he intended on staying a few more. It definitely looked like he was in transition. I wondered had he been living with a woman and got put out? Because almost all of his belongs were there.

Sterling laid back across the bed and I took my off my boots, then straddled myself on top of him. Looking down at him, he looked so unhappy, empty, and his eyes were so sorrowful. I rubbed his face.

"Sterling when was the last time you laughed?"

"Baby, it's been a while."

"Why are you so unhappy?" Sterling began to explain to me that he got caught up in some street garbage. I didn't believe what he was saying but I didn't push the envelope because the last time we had a touching moment I got quiet. I was just grateful for this alone time with him, and I didn't want to mess it up.

"Baby, I wish there was something that I could do to take the pain away." I said, Sterling didn't respond, he just looked away.

I tenderly rubbed Sterling's face and kissed his forehead. Sterling grabbed me by the sides of my face and pulled me closer to kiss me. We began to kiss and fondle one another. There was no electricity, the motions were measured and rehearsed. We undressed each other and had sex anyway with the absence of passion. We went through the usual motions, yet the sex was void. There were no sweating bodies, teeth grazing my shoulder blades, or heavy breathing. We had sex in just one position, and I didn't have an orgasm, which was a surprising first. What is really going on? I thought.

I knew Sterling's mind wasn't in the room much less on being with me, but I felt that giving him some ass was the least I could do since we were there and undressed. After Sterling came, he went and showered. He hadn't gotten in the shower immediately after sex since our first time together. It was obvious, he felt guilty for having sex with me.

The room was quiet when Sterling returned from the bathroom, he got in the bed, and we slept for a few hours. The sun began to rise, and Sterling said he needed to take me home because he needed to get some food to his sister. That was a bullshit lie because what could anybody be doing with food at 5 am and what food could he have to take to his sister from his truck that could not wait until a descent time of morning. I got dressed without questioning him. It was hard for him to look at me.

For most of the ride home, we didn't say much to one another. After a little word dancing, Sterling finally asked,

"So you know Drew?"

"Yes, we used to date many moons ago. I met him when he was at CU."

"I was at CU when he was there. So, what's up with you and Twist?"

"Nothing we are just friends. In fact, he treats me like I am one of his kids or something." I replied. Sterling just looked at me and nodded. This was an interesting line of questions from left field I thought because Sterling went back to being silent after he asked the questions. When we reached my apartment, Sterling didn't look at me or kiss me when he said goodbye. There was something going on with Sterling, did someone else have his attention? Was this his way of getting rid of me? Did he think I was hoeing around? I can't figure this out to save my life. I just got out of his truck and decided I would call him later.

As I was walking to my door, I didn't notice my car outside, which meant Brooklyn was not home yet. I guess things with her, and Ricky went well. It was 6 am on a Saturday, there was no chance that she was up yet, so I didn't call and check on her. I took a bath and got in the bed. I wanted to cry. I felt used. I refused to believe that not only was things between Sterling and I over, but the passion was gone too. After I woke up later that afternoon, I called Sterling, he didn't answer or return my call. I guess my assumptions were right. I wasn't ready to let him go yet.

Chapter X

My Aunt Gwen ran the kitchen at the Goal Post. She served the best rib tips in town. The kids were spending the weekend with my mother so turning the stove was senseless. I decided to pick up an order of rib tips to go. They would be the perfect meal to eat while I'm curled up on the couch to watch a movie. As soon as I made it to the kitchen window, Aunt Gwen grabbed me by the arm.

"Girl, I got something to tell you. I was over Pete's house braiding his hair yesterday when Sterling came over. He is about to buy a house with some woman. He kept on telling Pete that he doesn't love her and he isn't sure that he was doing the right thing, but he wants to buy a house and she has good credit. He listed reasons why he was hesitant about making that move with her. But he kept coming back to the fact that he was going to go ahead and buy the house with her. Sheridyn, he knows I am your Aunt so maybe he was talking to Pete about this in front of me because he knew

I would tell you and he wants you to stop him." Aunt Gwen said with excitement.

"Auntie Gwen you know how much I love Sterling, but he made a choice without looking at me as an option. He is where he wants to be with who he wants to be with. It doesn't seem like he was conducting interviews for the position, so that would lead me to believe love was the deciding factor. Sterling is simple, as long as he has cable, a stereo, and a bed, he could live anywhere, so there must be a reason why he doing this. Maybe he decided to talk about it in front of you because he knew you would tell me, and he wouldn't have to." I responded with a careless attitude. Aunt Gwen continued to persuade me to stop Sterling from buying a house with this other woman; I just didn't think it was worth the effort. After Gwen packed up my food, I left.

Yes, I cried when I got in the car. I guess it was finally over between Sterling and I. This was a familiar chorus, in my mind, where Sterling was concerned but this time, he made the choice. That would explain why the passion was gone the last time we had sex. The love for another woman quenched his desire for me. A 30-year mortgage is a hell of a commitment. I knew if Sterling made such a huge commitment it had to be because he was in love. He is not one to take a live-in girlfriend or buying a house lightly. I picked up my cell phone to call him, but I put it down before I finished dialing all seven digits. My heart was hurting. I loved him so much. Sterling had made his choice and I had to respect this woman as if I was in her position. As much as I didn't like it, I had to keep myself from calling him. I was broken hearted.

After about a month had passed, I gained the courage to call Sterling. I wanted him to tell me about his new living situation and hopefully, I would have the opportunity to make my intensions known to him.

"Hello sir, I am trying to get on your lunch calendar, what's up?" I asked.

"I'm a little busy, I just closed on a house a couple days ago, and I've been very busy moving." He replied. I thought he would tell me that he bought a house with another woman, but he didn't. I decided to push the envelope.

"When can we celebrate your new house, you know christen every room?" I asked,

"Sheridyn I can't see you. If I see you, I will not be able to keep my hands off you. I'm serious I can't see you."

"We have been together before and kept our hands to ourselves. Better yet, why don't you want your hands all over me?"

"Trust me it can't happen."

"Sterling how much trouble can we get into at a restaurant?"

"I don't care where we are, I will find a way to do it to you." Sterling exclaimed.

"Sheridyn, you know what. The only thing that separates man from animal is our ability to decide and the fact that we walk on two legs instead of four. All men cheat. Men are not meant to be with just one woman. Look at lions, elephants or any other wild animal. There is always just one male surrounded by females." Sterling said.

"Ok, why even be bothered then, why waste time pretending to love one woman?" I asked.

"It's just how we are. Don't get me wrong, we feel guilty as hell. During the ride home after we cheated, we feel like shit, but it is just who we are by nature."

I could not believe what Sterling was saying to me. Was this his subtle way of telling me he had a girl, and he would feel like shit after he slept with me?

"The fact that you are openly willing to cheat lets me know you aren't really in love. Sterling, I pray that one day you discover true love. See when you experience true love the thought of possibly causing your true love pain will supersede your desire to cheat." I responded.
Sterling didn't know the value of a good woman, so I continued,

"A woman adds increase and elevates a man. Whatever a man brings to the table, a good woman will give it back to him ten-fold. If you give a woman a seed, she will give you a child. If you give her a house, she will create a home. The tricky thing is you have only given me 10% of you and you have received 100% of me. Just think if you gave me 100% of you, what you would receive in return? You know God made woman from the rib of Adam. A woman is the rib of a man; she will protect his most vulnerable areas and stabilize him." My words didn't seem to matter to Sterling at all. I am not sure he was even listening to me. But I took that as his way of telling me to leave him alone.

I hung the phone up real confused. If he loved this woman so much, why was I still a temptress and why was he going out of his way to hide the fact that he was living with a woman? On the flip side, if she wasn't his true love then why did he buy a house with her? I had to call Twist to give me a man's point of view.

"I need to know why men choose women they don't really want then cheat, and then feel bad about cheating? Why don't they just be with who they love?" I asked. Twist chuckled before he answered.

"Ok, I'm gonna break it down for you. There are a few reasons why men do that. For some men, its insecurity, they don't believe that they are worthy of real love, so they are willing to settle for less than what they really need and want. For instance, a man may be attracted to blondes with big boobs, but they will marry a flat chested brunette, then cheat on her with a big breasted blonde. He does not feel that he can hold onto the blonde because everyone wants her. In some cases, a man has done so much dirt that he is scared that he is going to get back what he put out there. So, he is scared to love. He will only let his feelings go so deep, that way it won't hurt as bad when its time to give the devil his due. Then you just got the brother that is plain impatient. He will settle for a woman for the sake of having a female around. He doesn't love her. He is chooses her simply because she will put up with his shit." I could not believe what I was hearing before I could inject Twist continued,

"Also, you got the brotha that marries for the benefits that marriage brings. You know the societal status of being married, having dual incomes, he's ready to have kids, or getting married by a certain age is his goal. Sometimes a brotha gets married because the woman trapped him with a baby or pressured him so much, so he married her to shut her up. But I know what this is about, get over it, Sterling is not feeling you like that! He doesn't love you; he will never be with you."

"Thanks, I appreciate the talk, but I have never in my life heard such a crock of bullshit. Ok, I understand your theories, but why not be with the attractive, successful, woman that can cook and clean, that is good in bed, and have all the attributes that you desire? When a man opts to be with a woman that he doesn't love, he winds up hurting and damaging her by cheating. Why waste time and emotion when all along you know this ain't it? And, Sterling does love me; he is just scared to admit it." I replied.

"I will put it to you like this, a man would rather hold onto the old pick-up that is comfortable. It offers security, nobody else desires it or understands its value, nobody will steal it and it serves its purpose. A luxury car requires care, attention, maintenance, and everybody wants it. It requires more of an investment." Twist responded. My mind was blown. I wonder do men really think like this. I wish I could get a hold of the man's bible of excuses. I bet men could excuse away an excuse.

"I hate to tell you, but some men will choose the total package and still cheat, some men are just dogs." Twist concluded with a smile and a couple barks.

"Ok, bye Twist."

"Babygirl, I'm just trying to help you out." Twist and I hung up. He made my head hurt. I immediately called Madison to see what her take on the conversation was. I told her what Sterling and I talked about. She immediately replied,

"If Sterling loved that damn girl, he would be able to see you and not touch you or even think about it. That man knows damn well he don't want whoever he is with. He can only believe the lie that he is telling himself until he sees you. He knows he can't hide his love. I keep telling you I have seen you and Sterling together and that man can smell you walk in the room. Ya'll create such an energy when ya'll are together. Believe me when I tell you, you scare him. Seeing ya'll together scare me. Watching ya'll, made me believe in love again. You and Sterling look like what people that are in love should look like." Madison said. Everything she said I wanted to hear, but it didn't make me feel better inside.

"Well, Madison nonetheless, I am going to let it go."

"That's so sad to me, but ok. How long is this gonna last?" Madison asked. Madison knew me and Sterling's story better than anyone, so I tried to keep the hope alive, but with each passing week, the thought of me and Sterling getting back together became dismal.

I made it up in my mind that Sterling and I weren't destined to be together after all. Pete's advice was just to keep me on stand-by for Sterling. I decided to give up the thought. But as soon as I swore him off, I would randomly run into him again. This time, I saw him and the gang at First Friday. He was with the whole clan, including Drew. I felt like a ho or something by dating both Drew and Sterling, even though they didn't know each other at the time. Twist once told me that there was a small quantity of quality black men in Denver and the circles overlapped in one way or another. I know it is against man code to love someone that you know one of your boys slept with. Despite knowing a woman isn't a virgin, a man likes to think that he is the only one that has ever hit it. I had nothing to be ashamed of; I dated Drew many years before I met Sterling. I hugged them both. After walking off, I knew I was the topic of discussion. I felt so uncomfortable.

This was the first time I had been in this type of situation, and I knew my chances of being a couple with Sterling would diminish with every word they exchanged. I avoided the corner where they stood, but Drew made his way over to me.

"Sterling and I were over there talking about you. I told him that letting you go was the biggest mistake I ever made. You were so good to me. I was young and stupid. I regret letting you go more than I regret not going to the league. You know the funny thing about it is, I know I would have gone pro if you were in my life. Occasionally, my mom still asks about you. I told Sterling he is lucky to have you and not to screw it up because you are a good girl." Drew said.

"Thank you for those words Drew. It is nice to hear, but being a good woman has left me single. Being a good woman has caused the man I love to buy a house with another woman. I think I need to change who I am in order for someone to realize I am good for them and to them. Look at you Drew, it took you all these years, a bad relationship, and a couple of kids for you to realize that I am a good woman, but the fact remains you are still married to someone else even after your mother told you I was the one for you. That is the story of my life." I replied.

"Sheridyn listen to me; don't stop being who you are just to be with someone who can't appreciate being with you. The truth is, you threatened to leave me so many times, I never thought you would actually leave until one day, I looked up and you were really gone. I had no idea where to start looking for you. You know my boys accused you of being with me because I had a chance to go into the league, but my mother said the first time she met you, to hold on to you, but I listened to my boys instead of my mom. What's funny is they missed you too. They missed you cooking for us and stuff. They all ended up with gold diggers and I ended up unhappy. The one time I chose to listen to my boys instead of my mom cost me love." He said with a look of regret.

"By the way, it won't last." Drew said as he walked away. I had no idea what to say to Sterling, after all, he was living with someone else. Do I continue to pretend that I don't know he is a step away from marriage? I decided to just disappear into the crowd and sneak out. I didn't want to get embarrassed. I didn't want to accidentally have sex with him knowing it wouldn't mean a thing to him. Sterling was going to leave my bed and into the arms of his woman.

After leaving a function sponsored by the Mayor's office one evening, the finger food at the event just didn't hit the spot this time around so I decided to pick up some food from Greta's. I placed my order to go, only to turn around to see Sterling standing behind me. He greeted me with a smile and a huge hug.

"Let's have a drink." He said politely.

Sterling walked me to a quiet corner of the bar. I was ready to let him have it with both barrels when he said,

"Sheridyn I love you and I thought I was missing something. The streets were calling me, and I wanted them more than I thought I needed you. You never realize what you lost until you realize what you have. Every year, you mailed me a birthday card. This year, I didn't get a card from you, and I missed it. My birthday was just another day and to make things worse, I didn't get my card from you." Sterling said. As he continued to pour out his heart to me, all I could think about is if he feels this deeply for me, then why is he playing house with someone else? I just listened without saying a word.

The guy walked through the club selling flowers, Sterling bought two roses, he kissed one and gave it to me, he held the other one to my lips and I kissed it, he kissed it and held onto it. What was supposed to be a carry out dinner was turning into a date. We continued to talk. The magic between us was definitely back. Sterling looked straight into my eyes and said,

"You have always been good to me. I could never be with you though, because I would have to kill somebody behind you."

"Sterling, what do you mean by that? You should know I would never be unfaithful. You will always have the best of me." I reassured him.

"That's not what I mean." I didn't understand what he was leading to. Twist would have to decipher that for me later.

Sterling and I sat in a booth talking. I think he was trying to get the courage to tell me about his woman. Our conversation was just a bunch of small talk. I was so sad because I wanted to tell him that I loved him. I was not hurt that he chose someone else; I was hurt that he didn't even consider me as an option when he chose to settle down. A lady walked over to us and asked,

"You two look so much in love, can I please take a picture of ya'll?" That was funny, if she only knew the truth. I had on a suit and Sterling was in jeans and a t-shirt. We weren't even hugged up. I wonder what lead her to the conclusion that we were in love. We agreed to take the picture. I sat on Sterling's lap to pose for the picture.

"That is so cute. Thank you." She said. The lady noticed Sterling was wearing a cool and unusual screen t-shirt. She commented on how she liked his shirt. Sterling looked down at it, to remind himself of what he was wearing, and then he took it off and gave it to her. She was so elated, she offered to buy us a drink of appreciation, we both declined.

"You guys are such a cute couple; how long have you been married?" she asked. We both just smiled at her.

"We aren't married." I said.

"That's a shame you guys make a cute couple." She said as she walked away shaking her head.

I decided it was best that I left, Sterling still had me by the heartstrings, and I knew it would be hard for me to resist his advances and I wanted to give his woman the respect that I would want if I was in her place. Sterling walked me outside. Just as we walked out the door Jermaine walked up.

"What's up Sheridyn, Man you gone?" Jermaine asked.

"Naw, I will be inside after I holla at her."

"Alright man, see you inside."

Sterling walked me to his truck, so he could drive me to mine. He wanted my parking space because it was closer to the door. Before I got out of his truck, Sterling leaned over and kissed me. He pulled me on top of him as we continued kissing. This was a familiar tune, the same dance; this was just like our first kiss all over again.

"Sheridyn I want you, I need you now." He whispered. I tingled all over and I was beyond moist. My shirt was up and my pants were partially unfastened.

"I can't do this; we better not start this all over again." I said. I couldn't confess to him that I knew what was going on with him and this other woman. I think subconsciously, I thought if I didn't say it out loud, it meant the other woman didn't really exist. Our embrace wasn't coming to an end. I let down my guard and eagerly continued to kiss him. Out of nowhere, Jermaine started knocking on the window and yelling,

"Sterling, I know you are in there with Sheridyn doing something nasty. Get her titty out your mouth and open the door." We laughed as Sterling hit the button to roll down the window about two inches. Before we could say a word, Jermaine said,

"I don't know why ya'll won't go ahead and get married damn. That is a damn shame ya'll can't see each other without pawing all over each other. Sterling say goodbye and bring your ass inside and have a drink with yo boy." Sterling signaled to Jermaine to give him another minute, as he rolled the window back up, I fixed my clothes. Sterling turned back to me and said,

"Sheridyn can we continue this behind closed doors? I want you now. Let's go to your place." I kissed Sterling as I opened the door with my other hand and got out the truck.

"Bye, Jermaine is waiting." I said, before I shut the door. I was proud of myself. I actually said no to Sterling. I wasn't going to let him reduce me to a booty call. Sterling and I had been kicking it for a few years and this was the first time he asked to come to my house, so this was confirmation of his living situation. The other interesting thing was this was the first time he said he loved me.

Later that night, I called Racine to tell her about what happened. I finally told Racine what Aunt Gwen had told me about him buying a house with another woman. Racine replied,

"Yeah I used to run track with his girl. She does have it going on, she is sitting on a few dollars. In fact, the last time I saw him at the club, he told me not to tell his wife."

"Are they married?" I asked.

"No, but they might as well be." I was taken back by her response. Racine was supposed to be my friend and she was letting me make a fool of myself. I began to ask questions,

"Racine, is she tall, thin, my complexion and has braids?"

"Yeah, well she just got her braids taken out when did you see her?" I told her about the two times I saw her in Greta's. I was very hurt that Racine would keep something like this from me.

"Racine why didn't you tell me what was going on?"

"I wasn't getting involved, she is my friend and you are my friend what was I supposed to do?"

"Racine you ran track with her 10 years ago and haven't heard from her since then. You were with me when I gave birth to my son, how can you compare the two relationships? Racine, even if your loyalty isn't to me as a woman, how can you let her make a mistake like buying a house with someone you know doesn't love her and isn't faithful to her?"

"I just stayed out of it; I figured you both would learn your lesson. He asked me not to say anything, so I didn't."

"Why is your loyalty to him? How would you feel if your friend knew this information about your man and didn't share it with you?" I asked. Racine continued to say it wasn't her business. I just hung up on her.

She didn't see anything wrong with her behavior. We wonder why men are so sorry, why should we expect anything more from them when they have silly girls cosigning for them. Racine was officially off the team, friends like that are just enemies with ammunition and a point-blank shot. I couldn't believe she would betray me like this. I was so mad at Racine I could have screamed.

A few weeks later, I met my Aunt Gwen at the Goal Post so she could use my car for the weekend since I was having surgery first thing the next morning. Of course, I ran into Pete.

"Girl you look better than 60-weight gravy. Come over here and hug my neck." Pete said with a grin that only Pete had. Was 60-weight gravy a good thing? I wondered. Pete let off a couple of barks. Pete was a Q-dawg for life and made it known.

"Baby girl, can I buy you a drink? You know I can't have anything to drink, I am having surgery in the morning, and I can't have anything to eat or drink after midnight."

"Does Sterling know?"

"No I haven't talked to Sterling in awhile; we have gone on with our lives."

"I am sure he wants to know what is going on with you, especially something serious."

"Uncle Pete, I will be all right."

"Ya'll are creeping ain't ya'll? Tell the truth, ya'll are still kicking it."

"Sterling and I are completely done. He has a wife now."

"I know that ya'll have to still be doing your thing on the side and they ain't married."

"Whatever Sterling got on the side it ain't me. For real! Pete you know I love Sterling with all my heart but he made his choice to be with that girl, and I have to move on. I can't hold on to memories for the rest of my life."

"Sometimes men gotta do things for reasons other than love, but all men have one true love that they let get away and you are that love for Sterling."

"Uncle Pete I'm sorry I don't believe you. Why will a man settle for something less than true love?"

"Sometimes, we don't recognize a good thing because it's to close for us to see it. Man, love hurts and it's easier to be with someone that loves you, than to be with the one you love. You know Sterling is my man, my dawg believe me when I tell you, he loves you, always have and always will." Although Pete's words were comforting and encouraging, it wasn't enough to sway me into calling Sterling. If Sterling was concerned, he knew how to reach me.

A man walked up to the table as Pete and I were talking. After he spoke to Pete, he started checking me out and introduced himself to me. Pete looked at him and said,

"Naw man, no haps."

"That's you?" The guy said with a head nod.

"Naw dawg she people and she ain't available." Ok, I was too out done. It was ok for Sterling to live with someone, but I couldn't get my mack on? It was time for me to leave so I said goodbye to Pete and his friend. I hugged Pete and the guy asked if he could have a hug too, I just smiled.

"Damn, man she is fine, if that ain't you, your boy is slipping." The guy said as I walked away. All the way home, I thought about the conversation. Pete had given me something to hold onto, but was it enough to make me put myself out there to Sterling? I didn't like what I was feeling and being confused. I couldn't help but wonder, have I been chasing my tail all of these years?

Chapter XI

*A*fter returning to Connecticut, Madison kicked off her career as a poet and found a niche in acting as well. It was her turn to bring her son to see his father here in Colorado. She decided to mix business with this pleasure trip. She booked herself a few gigs during the couple of weeks that she would be in town. I was thrilled to see Madison again. I was excited because this would be my first time seeing her perform live. She sent a demo tape to a promoter that got her booked as the headliner at Club Zaire. The gig only paid $100, but she was allowed to sell her product as well. Club Zaire was the hot spot where special guests and local people could showcase their talent.

Madison or shall we say "Peaches" which is her stage name, performed a couple of pieces of spoken word from her newly produced CD *Thick like Peaches*. Watching Madison perform was like watching fish swim. She was definitely in her habitat. She performed with grace and ease. She had the crowd mesmerized and begging for more. She received a standing ovation as she walked back to her seat. The crowd requested an encore performance. The MC announced that he would bring her back up after she had a chance to wet her throat.

"Girl, that was so good, I am so proud of you. The baby don' grow'd up. My friend is fixen' to be a stara." I said as I hugged her.

"Child, I was so nervous because that second piece is new, I have never performed it before. So did you like it?" she asked as she blotted her forehead.

"Your poetry really engaged the crowd. You were all that, I just wanna know can a sista get an autograph before you blow up and forget the little people." I said with a smile.

"I'll still take your calls." Madison chuckled before sipping her water.

"I guess I need to gather myself and peddle a few CD's before the crowd spends all their money on liquor." Madison said as she pulled her product out of her small duffle bag to set up on a small table next to the stage.

"Sheridyn, is that Sterling over there with a boo?"

"Where? I don't see him. Are you sure it's him?" I asked.

"Girl, I am positive, take a gander at two o'clock." I casually looked over my shoulder to see Sterling and his boo at the table ordering their drinks. At this point, my feelings were hurt seeing him with another woman, even though we weren't dating, I just wasn't over him.

"I'll be back!" I said as I got up from the table.

"Girl, what are you about to do?" Madison said grabbing my arm as I began to walk away. I smiled and kept walking. I made my way up to the DJ booth and asked if I could get on the list of performers. Returning to the table, Madison asked,

"What did you go do? I got my cute shoes on tonight so I ain't trying to get in no consequences and circumstances with you."

"Trust me Madison, it's all good. Momma got this." I blended in with the crowd to make sure Sterling wouldn't notice me until I was already on stage. He really needed to hear me sing this song. After a couple of performers, the MC announced,

"Welcome to the stage, Lady Sheridyn, she is going to sing an original piece for us." Madison shook her head as I got up from the table. I began to sing.

"This is an original piece that I wrote about a man that is settling for a woman that he doesn't love, trying to get over the woman that he loves." I whispered as the music began to play. I adjusted the microphone and began to sing.

For a moment, Sterling was captivated with my presence. He had never heard me sing. I guess he didn't realize how caught up in the moment he was because the deeper I got into the song, the more entranced Sterling became. He almost completely turned his back to his boo. After concluding the song, the crowd went wild. I went back to our table to grab my purse. I smiled at Madison; she just shook her head as she autographed a CD for someone.

I went to the restroom to powder my nose. I freshened my lipstick in the bathroom mirror. Sterling's boo walked in. Without hesitation, she stood beside me and began speaking to me through the mirror,

"I am Victoria and more importantly, Sterling's woman. There is nothing you can do about that. I know he loves you. I know his face lights up whenever he sees you. He thinks about you sometimes as we lay on the couch watching television. I know when you are on his mind because he will laugh, look at me, then stop laughing without completing his sentence. I bet there are a million inside jokes that you and Sterling share, but he made the choice to be with me and not you. Loyalty will take me further than a look. So you can show up, sing, or whatever and it won't change a thing. You have his heart, but I have his mind, and body. The way I see it, 2 out of 3 ain't bad."

"Let me make sure I understand. You are confronting me because you rather live a lie instead of living life? I don't know where this conversation is coming from, but if you were so secure in your relationship with Sterling, we wouldn't be having this conversation now would we?" I asked arrogantly.

"Sterling may be a dog, but he comes home every night. You need to understand, you have love and I have loyalty that means you have what I want, but I have what you need. I guess that makes me the better woman because he chose me over you." Victoria stepped closer to me and continued,

"It hurts like hell knowing your image is etched in Sterling's mind for days after seeing you. He feels so guilty about still loving you, that he tries to compensate by being extra nice. I got karats, because he loves you. I hate to admit it; I like it when he sees you. I get gifts. Think about that!" Victoria said as she turned and immediately walked out of the bathroom. Returning to the table, Madison said,

"Girl you sang that song, I didn't know you had it in you."

"Thanks, but I was just told off in the bathroom by Victoria, Sterling's boo. That heffa had the gall to come in the bathroom and give me a piece of her mind then leave before I could respond. She told me I have what she wants but she has what I need."

"Such chudeness! You didn't hit her, did you?" Madison replied.

"No, I'm cool, I didn't hit her. That is why she darted out the bathroom so quickly. Heffa knew I would have let her have it. She got the nerve of Job though."

"Sheridyn, on the real though, I would rather be in your position than hers. I would not want to wake up next to someone for the rest of my life knowing that I am his second choice, knowing that he settled for me. I can only imagine my man seeing his first choice and him spending the next of couple days reminiscing about her. No, that ain't happening! See, I know what it feels like to sleep next to someone every night and still feel lonely, secretly wishing that each breath is the last breath because I wanted to be free but didn't have the courage to walk away. I thank God that you have been able to feel what you felt with Sterling because now you have a standard. For real though, if you and Sterling don't get married, I promise that would be a tragedy. I believe in my heart, ya'll are soul mates." Madison concluded.

I sure didn't feel like I had the better of the deal. Victoria was woman enough to stand up for her man and pull my ho card. I have to give her the credit she was due. I could have manned up and fought for him, but I refuse to make another woman become a casualty for a man's inability to decide. It was time for me to walk away from him. I know its time, but I can't. The interesting part to this evening was watching her pretend she wasn't bothered by my presence. Sterling spent the evening stealing glimpses of me when he could. And I tried to act like I wasn't bothered by their presence. I was happy when they finally decided to leave.

I guess it was time for me to give a relationship with another man one last college try. This loneliness was starting to get to me and it was very apparent that Sterling was content with who he was with. I didn't even know where the hot spots were to pick up men because I was out of commission for so long, but I was going to step out.

It was Saturday morning and I was up and out early to prepare for my night in the streets. First stop, the car wash. I had to get the manual labor out the way before I got my cute working. I was approached by a strapping young lad while I was washing my car and I was looking like I just woke up. He was a nice piece of eye candy, he had potential. Let's see if he is gonna ruin it when he opens his mouth.

"Babygirl, why your man ain't out here doing that for you? You gonna break a nail or something." He said as he began to unravel the vacuum hose. He looked like he had game, and he was just out to score some ass, but he might be cool to kick it with for a minute.

"If I had a man, believe me, he would be out here doing this or we will be doing it together." I answered.

"I am new to Denver, my job just transferred me here from KC, can you show me what's good in Denver?" I thought I should spit a little game back at him.

"I'm good in Denver what else do you need to see?" I said with a coy smile.

"Ok where you from."

"I live here but I am from Chicago."

"Damn, girl we are damn near neighbors, Kansas City is in Chicago's backyard. If you from Chicago I know that you are cool people then. Let me give you my number so we could hook up." He said. I turned away to get a pen and paper out of my car, when his cell phone rang.

"Excuse me baby girl, I gotta get this. *What's up, just chillin talking to this fine ass shorty up here at the car wash. Pete man, what's up for tonight? Where are we watching the fight? That's cool tell that punk ass Sterling he need to show up with a bottle. I think him and that fool Jermaine owe me from the last time we hooked up. Alright, I'll holla.* Sorry baby girl, here's my number, get with me later." He said. I accepted the number knowing good and hell well I wasn't going to call. He knew Sterling and the crew, so I was not trying to get caught up in no drama. I threw the piece of paper away without even looking to find out his name.

Later on, I met up with the girls to step out for the evening. As soon as we got to the club, I was approached by a man named Galen. He wasn't anything to write home about. We were the same height; he was clean cute, with almost a boy next door look about himself. Galen was funny and exciting. He was no Sterling but he could definitely fill in the gaps. Galen and I danced all night, as the club whined down, we exchanged phone numbers. Galen called me while I was driving home. We talked until the wee hours of the morning. The conversation ended with him asking me to attend a barbeque the next day. I agreed to go.

The next afternoon, I met Galen at his house. I was quite sexy. I had on a signature sundress and some sexy strappy sandals.

"Wow girl, you are fine as frog hair." Galen said as he greeted me at the door.

"Thank you, I think. Where is the que at?" I asked.

It's at my partner's house in Park Hill." Arriving at the house for the barbeque, we were greeted by Jermaine at the door. Jermaine looked at me and scratched his face. That let me know that Sterling was definitely there. Sterling and I made immediate eye contact from across the room, but I avoided him pretending that I didn't know him. Everything seemed all-good until Sterling caught me on the patio alone.

"So when did you and Galen start kicking it?"

"We aren't kicking it, this is our first date."

"Yeah me and Galen go way back. So what's up?"

"Nothing." I said and walked away.

I enjoyed the evening; Galen gave me my space by hanging with the fellas. I gravitated towards the ladies as if I had known them for ever. I frequently looked up to notice Sterling staring at me. It was as if he was making sure Galen and I weren't getting too close. I was so uncomfortable that I could not enjoy myself. I asked Galen to take me home because my babysitter had to get home early. The babysitter excuse is the best to get out of jail free card imaginable. Galen agreed, he was ready to go also.

Pulling up in front of my house, I told Galen that I had a great time and I enjoyed hanging out with him, but I could not see him anymore because of Sterling.

"Sheridyn, I don't understand why you can't talk to me?" Galen asked.

"I don't do friends. You and Sterling are boys and I don't want to be in a room and have slept with more than one man in the room. I am sorry, I have to draw the line somewhere and I like you too much to lead you on."

"He got somebody, that fool is practically married, you deserve to have somebody too. I never knew you were the same Sheridyn that he used to talk about. I think you are making a mistake if he wanted to be with you, ya'll would be together right now. Besides that, we don't kick it like that." Galen kept trying to convince me to date him by telling me all of Sterling's business, but I stood my ground.

Once again, I was confused about what I should do. This time, I decided to call a pow wow with the girls.

Madison was still in town, Brooklyn, Aunty Gwen; I even invited Racine to hang with us. They say keep your friends close, but your enemies even closer. Not that I was interested in Racine's advice or valued her opinion, I just wanted to know what she knew. All of us met for brunch on Sunday morning. Brunch was exciting; we laughed and talked like only the girls could.

"Ok, ya'll need to help a sista, what the hell am I gonna do about Sterling's raggedy ass? I have been waiting for him to get it together for years and it doesn't look like we have made any progress. If anything, we have taken a step backwards." Between the feedback from all of them, I am positive, I would be able to find some direction.

"Girl, I'm just gonna put it on out there. They go to Church with me and they look real cute together, they are engaged leave that alone and move on." Racine said without looking up from the French toast she was eating.

"I disagree, if he was so in love with that girl, he would not perk up and get all gitty when he sees Sheridyn. He can smell her walk in the room." Madison insisted. Aunt Gwen added in her two cents.

"I think Sterling is so handsome and ya'll just look like ya'll have so much fun when you are together." Once again, Racine interjected,

"I don't know why ya'll won't listen to me, they are practically married, she got it going on, he ain't gonna leave that. Not that you ain't got it together Sheridyn, but they dun bought a house and everything. I even think she got a ring; I will have to double check that next Sunday." I was more torn now than I was before we sat down.

"You know what? I am tired of being alone, so I am moving on. I don't care anymore. I am going to meet me a man that loves me and wants to be with me."

"You should be tired of saying that because I am tired of hearing you say that you are gonna walk away. Admit it girl that fool got you wide open." Racine said. I remained quiet because there was something to what Racine was saying. I don't know how many times I have told Sterling that I was going to leave him alone. I think he is just calling my bluff.

I set up brunch to get direction and clarity; instead, it turned into a sista friend discussion. I'm not complaining because it was great to catch up with the girls. I must admit, I can't remember the last time I laughed so much that my face hurt. For those couple of hours, I didn't think about Sterling. But when the laughing stopped, my thoughts drifted back to Sterling.

As much as I knew in my heart that Sterling didn't want to be with me, it was so much easier to hold on than it was to let him go. I wish someone would tell me what I was doing wrong and why I couldn't get his attention. Why wasn't I good enough? I questioned.

Chapter XII

I finally got the revelation that Sterling knew almost every eligible black man in the Denver metropolitan area. I needed to move on and the number of eligible men in Denver was dismal. I decided to try Internet dating, which was the easiest way to weed out men that knew Sterling. A couple of ladies at the office dated online successfully so why not try it? I had nothing to lose. I set up a profile on a singles' website. I enjoyed perusing through hundreds of pictures assigning background stories about the men based upon their pictures. I made a few contacts and even went on a few dates. I met more than my share of men. I met men who were looking for a wife and I met men that were just looking for a night. I even met the crazy society rejects. Nothing caught my attention.

After chatting and dating for about a month with no success, I was ready to give up. If this was all that Denver had to offer, I guess I need to relocate or get better acquainted with BOB. My battery-operated boyfriend. One day, I came across the most unique profile. This guy was distinguished, handsome, and extremely blunt. He was adamant about what he wanted and what he was unwilling to accept. I decided to drop him a line.

"Ok, are you angry, tired, or are you always this mean?"

"I'm not mean, I am just honest." He replied.

We chatted back and forth all afternoon. His name was Lawson Richardson. He had only been in Denver for two months. He relocated because his mother had a heart attack and she needed someone to take care of her. He wasn't crazy, he didn't know Sterling and if he was as cute in person as he was in his picture, then ladies and gentlemen we might have a winner.

Lawson and I exchanged numbers and started talking over the telephone immediately. He was intelligent, witty, and funny. We decided to meet for Happy Hour. He was quite attractive in person. He was15 years older than me, but I was ok with that because that meant he was ready to settle down and was sure about what he wants. Lawson was the ultimate gentleman. He didn't believe that a woman should touch a door in his presence. I loved the fact that not only was he a gentleman, but he respected me as a woman. I think he could be Mr. Right.

We set a date for the upcoming weekend. We talked everyday until Saturday arrived. I met him to drive to the casino. Lawson and I had conflicting schedules, so weekends were the only opportunity we had to spend time together, but we made the most of the time we spent together.

I wanted to do something different this weekend instead of dinner. I asked Lawson to take me to the circus; he was nowhere near interested in that. When I met him for dinner that evening, he surprised me with circus tickets. I was so excited; I appreciated that Lawson desired to see me happy. After the circus, Lawson said,

"I enjoyed myself, I am glad we went."

"I appreciate you taking me; I guess that means we got to do something you want to do now." Lawson stepped closer to me and said,

"Do you really want to do what I want to do?" I thought it was so cute that he was flirting with me, but I refused the advance.

"We aren't doing that, but I appreciate the offer." I responded as I took a step backwards.

"Well let's go to the casino?" Lawson suggested. Boys and girls, I think we have a problem. Did Mr. Right have a gambling problem? No God, no red flags. I thought. I was ready to cry. We have been to the casino at least once a week.

Driving to the mountains, Lawson and I sang. We were listening to the oldies station.

"Girl, you can carry a tune. I might have to marry you before you get famous."

"Please, I have never even considered singing professionally. Besides that, your opinion is bias, you like me a little bit."

"Correction, I like you a lot." We looked at each other and smiled. Arriving at the casino, we walked around.

"When Lawson asked me which casino did I prefer, I told him I didn't know there was a difference.

"Ok, we will go to my favorite place to play poker and you can play slots."

"That works." As we walked down the stairs Lawson stopped, turned around and said,

"You look great" and gave me a peck on the lips. I smiled and we continued down the stairs.

I sat at a slot machine near the poker table. I had to find a way to entertain myself because gambling is boring to me. I decided to watch Lawson play poker. I was clueless about the game, but after a couple of moments had passed, I picked up on it. At least enough to follow what was going on.

"Hold these" Lawson said as he handed me a hand full of chips and continued playing. Periodically, he gave me chips until finally he asked,

"Where are those chips I gave you?" I handed him all the chips. He handed my chips along with his to the dealer.

"Here, this is yours." Lawson said as he handed me two hundred dollars. Puzzled I asked,

"What is this for?"

"That's your money from your chips let's go." My stack of hundreds was smaller than the stack of hundreds he placed in his pocket. I assume he won and that was my share of the winnings, I wasn't going to ask any questions though.

The entire drive out the mountains, Lawson held my hand. At one point, he raised my hand to his mouth and kissed it. I thought that was sweet and endearing, I smiled at him. Lawson drove me to my car. We said our goodbyes underneath a streetlight. After he opened my car door, Lawson surprised me with a kiss. We embraced each other as we continued to kiss. I hadn't had a kiss like that since the last time I kissed Sterling. That was a perfect ending to a perfect night. Lawson insisted that I call him when I got home.

"Thank you for a wonderful evening."

"No, it was my pleasure; thank you for hanging out with me." Lawson sent me home with a smile on my face.

I had talked to Lawson's mother on the phone all the time but hadn't met her. One evening before Lawson and I headed out for dinner, he invited me to the house to meet his mother. His mother was 84 and the cutest old woman you could imagine. She was maybe 4'11 on a good day and didn't look a day over 60. Her age was only apparent when she talked, moved, and how she dressed. I fell in love with Ms. Pearl. I called her Ms. Pearl, but she insisted that I call her mom. I would sit at her kitchen table and talk with her until Lawson would steal me away to the basement or whisk me out the door.

I was glad I had Lawson in my life. I was a little scared about getting too close to him. I just knew that he was too good to be true. I had been sick for a few months; Lawson was unaware of my issue. My doctor told me a hysterectomy was inevitable. I could not put off the surgery any longer. Some men think having a hysterectomy takes away from a lady's womanhood, so I didn't want to tell Lawson but my health was declining and I couldn't function. Lawson invited me out; I could not go because I was feeling that bad. Just to make it eight hours I had to take 1600 mg of ibuprofen.

Hiding my illness became harder and harder. After being rushed to the emergency room, my doctor indicated that I could no longer postpone the surgery; my life was now in jeopardy. I was forced to tell Lawson what was going on. The fact that I was having a hysterectomy didn't faze him. Lawson called every few days checking on me during my six week healing process, asking did I need anything. I refused to let him come by. I didn't want him to see me looking less than my best. I was surprised he stayed persistent.

My healing process was over. I was back up and around. My doctor asked me how sex was going for me. I told him I hadn't tried it; I was scared to. When I told Lawson what the doctor said he was more than willing to help me out with the doctor's prescription. Lawson and I had been seeing each other for more than six months and we had not had sex. He was patient and understanding.

My life was back on track, moving at a million miles a minute. It was virtually impossible for Lawson and I to catch one another on the phone much less see each other. We played so much phone tag that our relationship was based on a stream of voicemails. My message said,

"Lawson, I am fed up, I want a divorce you get the dog and the kids, and I will keep the house and the car."

"This is your husband I have been trying to serve you with divorce papers, but my attorney can't find you." He responded. That was our inside joke, he called me wifey and I called him husband.

Lawson was a little stuck in his ways. He thought a man should do the proper thing and pick up a woman from home not just meet at a location, like we had been doing. I told him that I was conservative about letting men meet my children. We had been seeing each other for more than six months, I guess it was time. I finally invited him over for dinner and let him meet the children. He enjoyed hanging out with us. Lawson was proud that he got to meet my children because he knew how sacred they were to me.

Dating Lawson was great; I felt how much he loved me. It seemed that he lived solely to keep a smile on my face. I mentioned to him that I wanted to see a movie that had just been released. He surprised me by taking me to the movies on our next date. This was a big deal because he hated going to the movies. He held my hand during the movie and stole small kisses between scenes. I was on cloud nine. I felt like I was the only thing that mattered to Lawson. Much to my surprise, Sterling had not crossed my mind, but almost a year had passed, and I hadn't heard from him either.

I decided to surprise Lawson for his birthday and take him to dinner. I put on my sexy, strapless, black dress and I asked him to wear a suit. This was my first time seeing him in a suit. Damn, that man can hang a suit! There was a brief wait when we arrived at the restaurant, even though we had reservations. As we stood waiting for our table, Lawson continuously kissed me on my temple. I smiled each time he did it.

"You keep doing that just because you want to see me smile." I said.

"Yes, I love to see you smile." Lawson said as he kissed me again. The waitress complimented us on how well we looked together. I presented Lawson with his gifts. He was pleased. I received a kiss on the forehead as a token of appreciation.

Lawson and I did not have the fire and passion between us that Sterling and I possessed, but I enjoyed every moment that I shared with Lawson. Although there was a significant age difference, Lawson and I had a lot in common. I knew my role as a woman, and I enjoyed Lawson treating me like one.

Lawson had become acclimated to Denver, although he missed DC. He had a consulting firm that he was trying to get off the ground. He worked a job at night and worked on his business by day. I introduced him to some of my business connections and helped him in every way that I could. We seemed to make a great team. We recognized that added value of being a part of each other's lives. Before I realized it, my relationship with Lawson turned into a business partnership.

Lawson and I weren't dating anymore, and we only talked about business. He even started paying me for helping with his business. I thought it was my duty as his girlfriend to ease his load so that we could have more time to spend together, but the more I helped him, the less frequent our dates became.

"Sweetie, you don't have to give me a commission. I am honored to help you grow your business."

"Sheridyn, I want you to remember this, your education cost you, so your knowledge should cost other people." I was puzzled and Lawson recognized it.

"Let me put it to you another way, you paid for your education when you went to school, don't let nobody pimp your knowledge. If I wasn't paying you for your help, I would have to pay someone." Lawson said gave me a courtesy kiss on top of my head. I understood what he was saying. Lawson wasn't very romantic, but he was extremely practical.

Chapter XIII

Once again my damn phone was ringing after 9. Looking at the caller ID, I saw that it was my mother, what could she possibly want this time of the night, I wondered. Reluctantly, I answered the phone, "Yes ma'am?"

"I was calling to tell you about Pete, he died about an hour or so ago."

"Pete who?"

"Pete, Pete."

"Not Uncle Pete."

"Yes Uncle Pete."

"No way mom what happened?"

"Well, I guess he went home to South Carolina for the holidays. He caught pneumonia, one thing led to another, and his kidneys began to fail. They put him on dialysis. He was doing better, then about an hour ago, his kidneys gave out completely and he passed. His father just called us at the bar."

"Oh my God mom that is so sad. I can't believe Pete is gone. Thanks, mom, for calling me."

When I hung up the phone, Sterling was the first thought that popped into my mind even before the reality that Uncle Pete was actually gone. My heart hurt for Sterling. I just wished I could have comforted him. I hesitated for a moment. What should I do? I didn't want to disrespect his girl or add any other turmoil to his situation by calling, but I wanted him to know that I was here if he needed me. I began to pray silently because Pete was not only a friend to Sterling, but he was also somewhat of a mentor. They had known each other for more than 15 years. Despite the decision Sterling had made, I thought it was important that he knew I was an outlet if he needed one. For some reason, I still felt connected to him.

I took the cowards approach to the situation and sent a text message. *I just heard about Pete, I am so sorry. You* and *Derrick are in my thoughts and my prayers. Please call if I can do anything to ease this troubled time.* I knew there was a possibility that he may not get the message tonight, but at least he would know that I made an attempt.

Over the next couple of days, the memorial details began to unfold. The different clubs were having fundraisers in Pete's honor. The service for his family and his body would be laid to rest in South Carolina. A second Memorial service for his friends would be held here in Denver a few days later. I sat and debated if I should go to South Carolina. I didn't know what I should do. I called Madison to ask for advice. After I told her what happened she said,

"I think you should go, if not for you, go for Sterling. It will comfort him to see you there. You can easily avoid his boo. If I had to choose between this one and the one in Denver, I would choose the one in South Carolina. That is where Sterling will need your presence the most. Follow your heart."

After listening to Madison and digesting the whole situation,

"You convinced me, I will book the arrangements immediately." I said. I thought about calling Sterling, but it was easier if I just went. I knew that there was a chance that Sterling's boo wouldn't go to South Carolina because that was more intimate for the family and closest friends. If Sterling and I were together I would not have went so he could have some private time to reminisce and grieve with the fellas. Reality was, there was no way that I would attend the services here in Denver. I just wasn't ready to see Sterling being comforted by another woman.

I got enough courage to book a flight. The entire plane ride, I second-guessed myself. Was I overstepping my bounds? Would Sterling think I was out of order for coming? After all, Sterling had not returned my call, text, or called me to even let me know Pete had passed. It was too late for doubt, I couldn't turn back now. I was mourning for Sterling's loss rather than the fact that Pete was gone. Pete meant a lot to me, but I know he was like a right arm to Sterling, the thought of surviving without Pete would be hard.

After checking into the hotel, I thought about calling Sterling a million times to let him know that I was in town. I was so afraid of how he would react. I have never invaded Sterling's personal space until now. I have shown up without an invitation, I was really on edge. I don't think Sterling would react negatively to my presence; I just didn't want him to feel uncomfortable.

My nerves kept me awake all night. As I got dressed, I took a deep breath and headed to the funeral hoping I was doing the right thing. Arriving at the church, I sat in the car nervously twitching trying to find the courage to get out and go inside. I had flown all this way, yet I was still apprehensive, I didn't know what to expect. I was alone and I didn't know who was who. I didn't know if Sterling's girl would be here either. Would she act a fool? Would there be some baby momma drama because I was the female that no one knew. There were so many variables that caused me to fidget even more. Ok, I had to get my mind together. My imagination was getting the best of me.

I watched from a distance as the family began to form the processional and enter the church. After everyone had entered the church, I took a deep breath wondering was this the right thing to do? I had come too far to turn around now. I exhaled and got out the car. After all, what is the worst that could happen? I timidly walked inside the church where it was close to capacity with people in mourning.

I only recognized the pallbearers. Most of them I had met at the club with Sterling and Pete before. The pallbearers sat solemn with tears streaming down their faces. I slid onto the last pew closest to the door. I caught a glimpse of Sterling as he sat wiping tears from his face. He sat among the other pallbearers trying to remain strong. He looked so handsome, yet gloomy. I wished I could have just laid his head in my lap and let him cry.

I felt Sterling's sorrow from a distance as the service progressed. The minister delivered the eulogy then extended the opportunity for people to formally speak words of expression to the family in memory of Pete. Without thinking about it, I jumped out of my seat and headed to the front of the church to make my remarks. Once I realized what I was about to do, there were two people that preceded me and 3 people were behind me, it was too late to turn back.

Everyone before me expressed tear filled notes of goodbye, what could I say that would comfort I thought?

I removed my dark sunglasses as the usher escorted me to the podium. Looking at Sterling on the front row breathing hard trying desperately to hold back the tears, I began to speak.

"Uncle Pete, as I affectionately called him and he called me Baby Girl, I think mostly because he could never remember my name. Every time I saw Pete, he made sure I hugged his neck. I always was guaranteed to be greeted with a smile, a kiss on the forehead, and sent away with words of wisdom that I always found to be encouraging and comforting."

At that point, my voice must have sounded familiar to Sterling because he looked up at me for the first time. The other pallbearers looked at Sterling then at me with a smile. I continued,

"I think about Pete, and I know that I am not alone when I say none of us have anything bad to say about him. The last time I saw Pete he said, *baby girl you look as good as pot liquor.* I still don't know if that was a compliment or not." The crowd chuckled lightly. I noticed the tears on Sterling's face begin to dry up as I spoke,

"I didn't know Pete as a brother, son, father, or lover, but I knew him as a friend and I am not here to mourn his death but celebrate the fact that I was privileged enough to have known him. Someone once said, i*t's not what you leave for your loved ones that matters, it's what you leave in them that's important.* As I look around this room today, I see a broad range of people varied in age, sex, race and relationship, that Pete impacted leaving a legacy of heartfelt love. As the tears continue to dry, let the funny moments, kind words, and loving memories of Pete permeate your hearts. To the family, continue to anchor yourself in the comfort of the Lord. Pete isn't gone, he left. He left his memory etched in our hearts. He left his smile branded in our minds. He left laughter in our souls. He left us with the richness of who he was. I am positive every one of his friends and family members has a *I remember Pete… or this one time Pete…* story that will cause us to burst into laughter even on this day of his home going. Be encouraged."

Before turning to leave the podium, I looked at Sterling and gave him a comforting smile, he nodded back at me. Rather than returning to my seat, I walked directly into the foyer, signed the book for the family, and left a card with the usher. I moved so quickly I never noticed how anyone responded. Once I got to the car, I realized how fast my heart was beating and how out of breath I was. I don't know what I was afraid of. I accomplished what I came here to do. I called Madison and told her how things went.

"See I told you there was nothing to worry about." That was easy for her to say. I am just glad I remembered to wear deodorant. I'm glad I got outta dodge before anything happened.

I wanted to give Sterling something special for his birthday this year. With Pete's funeral being a couple of weeks before Sterling's birthday, I thought he needed something more than a card. I wanted to give him a special gift that when he saw it, he would think of Pete not me, and of course something that he could take home and not have to explain. Madison and I entered a major brainstorming session to come up with the perfect gift. A gift should not cause this much brain damage I thought, but nothing seemed appropriate.

One afternoon, as I searched my personal files to retrieve my tax information, I came across a series of pictures that I forgot I had. There were pictures of me, Racine, Pete, Derrick, and Sterling that none of them had ever seen before. That would be the perfect gift. Lucky for me, I always get double prints. I had the pictures of just Derrick, Pete, and Sterling matted and framed. This was the perfect gift. All I needed was a card and everything would be perfect. I spent an hour in the store picking out a sympathy and birthday card.

Once I assembled everything into a nice gift presentation for Sterling, I called him. I reached his voicemail, *Hey Sterling, it's Sheridyn. I know you aren't into celebrating your birthday this year, but I have a package for you. Call me so we can meet or give me an address where I can send this. Talk to you soon.* He never returned my call. I tried a couple more times over the next several weeks, I never heard from him, so I packed away his gift. My feelings were hurt because I assumed I meant more to Sterling than this. He said he missed not getting a birthday card from me last year, but this year, he is avoiding me like the plague. To make matters worse, he hasn't taken the time to see if I was ok after Pete's death.

Six months had passed, I still hadn't heard from Sterling. It was even more shocking that I hadn't ran into him either. I prayed that he was well, and that Pete's death hadn't had an adverse affect on him. Sterling was already a heavy drinker. I was praying that nothing bad happened to him. It was really hard to believe that Pete was gone for real. There were days I still hoped to run into him for advice.

I decided to do something different with the children and take them to the carnival in our City Park. The grown folks sat and listened to live jazz while the teenagers visited booths and looked around. I was sitting in my lawn chair under a shaded tree when I noticed Sterling. I waited for a moment to see if his girl was close by before I approached him. I wasn't trying to hug him and get hit in the back of my head by his woman. After the coast was clear, I got out of my chair and walked up to him, he was standing with his entourage of friends.

"How are you sir?" I said with a smile. Sterling's face lit up.

"Damn baby how have you been doing? Where have you been?" He asked as he hugged me tightly. I was uncomfortable with him hugging me so tightly and lingering in my arms because we were in public, and I was still watching out for the potential psychotic girlfriend. Sterling continued to hold me closely and squeeze me.

"I ain't even trying to hear that, you haven't thought about me. I have called you several times over the past few months and you haven't called a sista back. You are so quit." I said with a chuckle. There was no excuse of why Sterling had me on radio silence but he offered a frail excuse.

"Sheridyn in real life, I have had a lot of shit going on, you just don't know." Sterling never took his arm from around me as we talked.

"Well, I have a package for you." Sterling looked at me, licking his lips.

"What you got for me?"

"See there you go, you always trying to do it to me."

"You like it when I do it to you."

"I do but not right now."

"I got some things that I think you might want. The package has some pictures and stuff that I have been holding since your birthday. Give me an address and I will drop it in the mail, or I can send it to Derrick's job? Better yet, if it works for you, give me a call next week sometime and we can meet." Sterling took his arm from around me and said.

"Oh hell naw! You got to be kidding me. Are you that busy that I have to make reservations a week in advance?" I laughed at him as I spoke to his friends and introduced myself to the ones I didn't know. Sterling was looking at me with dismay.

"Damn it's like that?" He said as he turned to greet by passers.

"Quit crying, ok let's get together Wednesday."

"Hell, its Sunday why I got to wait 4 days?" Sterling exclaimed.

"Damn bruh you must have lost big daddy status for real; you are on a four day turn around time." Jermaine interjected. Sterling continued to speak to people passing by as a way to pretend he was ignoring me. But it was obvious that he was pouting.

"Sterling, its not that you aren't important to me, I just have some things going on this week." He looked over his shoulder and rolled his eyes at me.

Sterling's feelings were hurt that I put him off for a few days. I was glad to see him; I just was not going to manipulate my schedule to accommodate him. Sterling threw his hands up in the air,

"Damn, like that. I gotta wait til Wednesday? Do I need to call your secretary to confirm too?"

"No sir, I will call you Tuesday and confirm. You still got Big Daddy status." I said with a wink.

"Like hell I do." He said as he walked away. His feelings were really hurt. This scene was too funny to me. I haven't exchanged two words with Sterling in close to a year and I was supposed to jump up and down because he decided to bestow his time upon me. Wrong answer hot dog!

I decided that I would rub his face in it a little more. Sterling was still in sight when my daughter came begging me for money.

"Camiyah come here I want you to meet someone." We walked up to Sterling. "Camiyah this is Sterling an old friend of mine. Sterling this is my daughter Camiyah."

"Nice to meet you Camiyah, you are pretty just like your mom."

"Thank you but I am prettier than my mom." Camiyah said sarcastically.

"You sure are and I bet you don't make your friends wait four days when they want to hang out with you like your mom does. How old are you anyway?"

"I am fourteen, oh yeah my mom is just shady like that."

"Gee thanks Camiyah." I said as she walked away.

"Damn girl she looks just like you."

"Are you still crying or will Wednesday work for you?"

"Whatever." Sterling responded as he turned his back to me again. I chuckled and walked away.

Tuesday, I called Sterling to confirm our Wednesday meeting, he didn't answer the phone, I left a message, and he didn't return my call. Sterling wasn't a man known for his word being bond. Wednesday afternoon, he finally called to get with me.

"Sterling I didn't hear from you so I made other plans. I will call you tomorrow to see if we could get together."

"Oh it's like that?"

"Like what? Sterling I don't know why you are all hurt about this. I have been trying to deliver this package to you for more than six months now."

"Ok, just call me tomorrow. We can meet after my drug and alcohol class." He said abruptly.

Thursday afternoon I called, but I got his voicemail. *Sterling, Sheridyn, call if you are still available this evening.* This time, he promptly returned my call. We decided to meet at the Take Five, a pool hall that was a half way point for both of us. I walked in Take Five to find Sterling already at the bar. We hugged and he kissed me on the forehead. He introduced me to the bartender. After ordering drinks I had to ask.

"Ok, let me see if I understand, you just left drug and alcohol class to meet me for a drink?"

"No offense, but next to pussy, liquor is the best thing you can give a brotha after drug and alcohol class." He replied.

"No offense taken, but is that your round about way of asking for some?"

"Only if that is your round about way of offering some." We both laughed.

"Why are you attending those classes? Did you get a DUI?"

"Yep, I had to go to DNA classes for two years; I still got six months left. I go every damn Thursday." I just shook my head.

"Hell, what are you getting an associate degree in drug and alcoholism?"

"I was thinking the same thing, not only do I have to go to the classes; they are hitting a brother deep in his pockets to attend this class." I just shook my head.

"Ok, time to see your big boy prizes." I said with excitement. I pulled out the slightly worn manila envelope with a picture frame hanging out of one end of it. First, I handed Sterling the frame. He looked at the frame and started laughing,

"Man when did we take these pictures? Where did we take these pictures? Wait a minute; they weren't all taken on the same night, were they?"

"No." I reminded him of the evening we took the pictures.

"Sheridyn look at my man Pete. It's so hard to believe he is really gone. Check out Derrick, man I forgot we took these pictures. Wait, this was when Derrick first had his surgery huh?"

"Yes."

"Man we were tore up weren't we? Look at Derrick, he just had open heart surgery and he's in the club looking like new money and faded as hell." I reached into the envelope and pulled out other shots.

"I didn't frame these because I knew you couldn't take them home because Racine and I are in them, but I wanted you to see them anyway." Looking at the pictures, he started laughing and put them in his shirt pocket.

"Man, I remember this night; we were over at Jackson's in these and Club Delite in these." Sterling chuckled as he spent a few moments reminiscing and chuckling about the evening we took the pictures.

"I was going to pack up everything and send it to Derrick's job if I hadn't ran into you."

"Sheridyn, I would have never seen my package if Derrick got his hands on it first. My frame would have been posted up in his house like it was his. Hell, I'm gonna have to find a place to put it in my own damn house, where that fool won't steal it."

After Sterling finished reminiscing about the nights the pictures were taken, I handed him two cards, a birthday card and a sympathy card. I also included a poem someone had sent me across the internet. He read the birthday card.

"I like this card did you write it?"

"No I bought it. I know you were feeling down with Pete dying just a couple weeks before your birthday. I wanted to give you something special."

"You are kidding me; this card fits us. Thanks." He opened the sympathy card and a letter I had written him fell out. He immediately stuck the letter in his pocket.

"You aren't going to read it?"

"Not now, I will read it when I get home."
Sterling read the sympathy card and began to recant how he found out about Pete's death.

"Sheridyn I had just talked to Pete the day before he died. He said he was going to be all right, he just had gotten a hold of some bad pussy. You know Pete kept pussy on the brain. Pete could make a joke in any situation. Check this out, my brother got the call first and he picked up Max and Jermaine. It was about ten o'clock that night when them fools came knocking on my door. I opened the door to see 3 grown men crying. I knew it was Pete. We cried at my place for a minute, and then we started going door to door knocking on all the homie's doors, one at a time delivering the news in person. In real life, Pete was a brother to me." Tears began to develop in Sterling's eyes as he rubbed his hand across the framed photo of Pete. I was just talking to him last night. I can't believe these pictures. Man, we used to have fun."

"I went to South Carolina because best friends can't be replaced, but I wanted you to know that I am available as a substitute. If you need an ear, a shoulder, a place of rest and comfort, know that I am here for you. I know you have a girl, and it wasn't my place to be at the funeral, but I know in your time of need in the past, you were able to find comfort in me. I mourned you when Pete died, I didn't mourn his death until later. I couldn't bring myself to attend the memorial service in Denver. I didn't want my presence to cause you any more heartache. I decided to give you something that would capture who Pete was and you could preserve it for ever." I said as I rubbed Sterling's shoulder.

"This means so much to me because I lost my house, and my entire box of pictures was thrown out. I have no pictures of family or friends, so I really appreciate this.

"What happened to you in South Carolina? You were there then you disappeared faster than a New York minute."

"I didn't belong there, but I went for you. I had to get outta Dodge before drama popped off." Sterling hugged me and kissed me on my temple.

"I was trying to give you some space and respect your girl. That is why I have limited my contact with you." I said.

"My girl and I was so through by the time Pete died, you see she wasn't there." He responded.

"I really didn't pay attention; I just wanted to pay my respects and get out of there." Sterling leaned over and kissed me on the forehead again,

"Thanks, I know the perfect spot that I am going to put this picture. I already know Derrick is going to try and get it from me."

"Can I have my other pictures back, the ones you stuck in your pocket?"

"Naw, these are mine too." Sterling said. We continued to talk basically, playing catch up.

"Sterling let me ask you something. Do you know why the love we made was so good? It was because I loved you so much. Every time I made love to you, it was from my heart to yours. Let's face it, ass is just what it is, ass. You'll get out of it whatever you put into it. What we had was real and pure. I didn't have a place in your life, so I settled for a place in your bed until I could get a place in your heart. The only way you allowed me to express my love to you was in the one area that you permitted me in which was your bed." I continued,

"You want to know something funny; I knew the exact moment that I lost you."

"When?"

"Remember that night you were almost in the accident?"

"Yeah, I was tripping that night for real."

"Well, as I massaged you to get you relaxed, you turned around and basically let me know that I touched a deep, intimate, and tender part of you. A place that you weren't willing to share with me, I scared you away. I wanted to tell you then that I loved you. I was afraid to tell you because I was scared of the rejection. Pete and I talked about it that was when he told me to stop having sex with you."

"Oh, he did, that's my man." Sterling said with a smile.

"Because of where we started you could never see me in any other position. No pun intended. You never wanted to see that there was more to me than what existed in the bedroom. Little do you know my best traits are outside the bedroom?" Sterling nodded without looking up at me. He sipped his beer. I wondered what he was thinking. Was I being a fool by opening myself up to him again? I was also wondered if he and his girl weren't together anymore why had been avoiding me over the past few months.

Sterling and I sat at the bar talking for the next couple of hours reminiscing about our favorite memories of Pete and the best of times we shared. It was like we were getting to know each other for the first time.

"You know Sterling, Pete is the one that told me you loved me."

"Oh, he did, did he? You know he used to call me whenever you were at the club to let me know that you were there looking good." Sterling responded.

"The ironic thing is it was Pete that made me hold onto loving you. If it wasn't for him, I would have given up on you a long time ago." Sterling just smiled.

Sterling and I ran out of things to talk about because we really didn't know what to say to each other. This was our first real conversation in over a year. I was afraid to ask him questions and he was afraid that would ask questions. That only meant it was time to go.

As we walked out the club, we stopped to talk to the bouncer. We engaged in small talk. The conversation was getting lengthy.

"Well fellas I gotta go, I got black eyed peas and greens at home waiting for me." I said as I stepped forward to hug Sterling goodbye.

"Ok I have to eat take out or whatever and you eating like that. You couldn't bring a brotha a plate." Sterling said.

"I figured your girl would be hooking you up." I replied.

"I told you I live like a bachelor."

"Well I didn't know that until now. You gotta speak up on things like that."

Sterling gave the bouncer a pound as we walked out the door. Sterling parked closer to the club's entrance than I had. He decided to drive me to my truck rather than walking me to the other side of the building. I gave Sterling a hard time about not having gas in his truck. In the seven years I've known him; I have never known him to have more than a quarter tank of gas at one time. We chatted about nothing to delay the inevitable goodbye. Just like our first date, neither one of us really wanted the night to end.

"What you know about this?" Sterling said as he turned up the volume of his stereo.

"Quit playing, baby you know that's my girl Anita. Try again; you might have to go a little deeper to stump a sista." Sterling began to sing. I watched him silently with admiration. Sterling and I got out of his truck to walk me to mine. The music continued to play in the background.

"It was great seeing you again sweetheart, thank you so much for my stuff." Sterling said as he held me close. Adoringly, he began to rub his chin across my head. Hesitantly, Sterling rubbed his face along the side of my face as he held me. He leaned in with apprehension and kissed me. We kissed slow and gently. It has been over a year since Sterling and I had touched each other but even then, we were at a place of familiarity. Our simple embrace quickly turned passionate. We kissed, with our bodies in sync; we affectionately moved our hands across each others bodies. Sterling ran his fingers through my hair. As the kiss heightened, he firmly gripped my butt and with his other hand, he tenderly rubbed my breast. The kiss became more personal. I breathed heavily as he rubbed his hand between my legs. Headlights shined in our general direction, so we let go of each other. We were speechless. Was this a preamble to a new masterpiece of love? I thought.

Sterling and I shied away from verbal expressions of emotions. After all of these years, we have never had a conversation about "us." Rather than talking about what just had happened, we avoided the subject by getting competitive. That was one of the weirdest elements of the relationship that Sterling and I had. We would avoid talking about the obvious with trivial conversation. To prolong the goodbye, I asked Sterling about Max because I hadn't seen Max in years.

"Man I am suing Max. I have this little painting business on the side that I am getting off the ground. We painted Max's house for him, and now this brotha don't want to pay us. Even after we discounted the price because he is people."

"I'm sorry to hear that I know that was your boy. Hopefully ya'll will work it out before it gets ugly."

"So you know there is another Deuce movie coming out?"

"Yeah, let's go see it together."

"Have you seen the trailer? It looks funnier than the first one."

"Let's make it a date; you know nobody finds that movie as funny as we do." As we made plans, the subject of his girl never came up or what happened with that. We made plans to see each other the next day so that he could come and get a plate for dinner. We hugged and said goodbye for real this time. The next day, I called Sterling to come get his plate; he said that he would come get it the following day. He never called back or came by.

A couple of weeks later, I called Sterling to confirm our opening night date to see Deuce's movie, he never returned my call. I was done. Sterling had proven that he didn't want me and he wasn't a man of his word. Sterling has never been the love of my life for years, but it is getting old.

Chapter XIV

I frequently thought about Sterling, but I wouldn't call him. I hoped I would run into him because I really wanted to see him. I finally broke down and called him.

"Hey, what you got going on tonight?" I asked.

"I am kicking it with the fellas this evening to watch the fight, what's up with cha?"

"I wanted to come through, watch a movie or something."

"Well, I will holla at you when I leave my boy's house."

"Ok that's cool." I was looking forward to seeing him, but deep inside, I knew he wouldn't come through. Much to my surprise, Sterling called around 11 pm.

"What's up baby? Things are winding down now; do you still want to come through?" Sterling asked.

"Naw it's too late, I am already in bed, just get at me tomorrow."

"I'll do that, have a good night baby."

The next morning, while I was getting dressed for church, I received a text message from Sterling. *Call when you get out of Church.* I didn't reply to the message I just called after Church. Surprise, surprise there was no answer; I didn't bother leaving a message. I followed my normal Sunday routine which was to eat and take a nap. After I woke up from my nap, Sterling called,

"What's up with you?"

"Just woke up, what's going on."

"You wanna come through?"

"Yeah, but you sound like you are on your ass?"

"Yeah, baby I drank way too much last night, but I'm good."

"We can reschedule."

"Naw come on through. I'll be alright."

"Ok, I am on my way, do I need to bring anything? Are you hungry?"

"I'm alright, see you in a minute." Before heading over, I stopped at the grocery store to get some fried chicken from the deli and something to drink. Arriving at Sterling's house, he was laid out on the sofa watching the game.

"I brought some chicken wings if you want some. Who's winning?" I said while I took off my shoes.

"Chicken sounds great, the AFC is getting whopped."

"Who are you going for?"

"I am betting on the NFC." We watched the game in silence for a while. I sat on the love seat, and he continued laying on the sofa eating the wings.

"This chicken is pretty good; you got this at the grocery store?"

"Yeah."

"I'm gonna have to check them out. This game is a wrap; let's go to my room so we can watch a movie." Sterling suggested.

We went upstairs to his bedroom. I smiled when I saw the framed picture of Pete that I gave Sterling a year ago, set up in his room with his Bible. I got positioned in the bed as he called out movies to see what I wanted to watch.

"I haven't seen any of them so whatever you think is fine." I responded.

"Ok, I will put in this movie, it is funny as hell." After putting the movie in, he got in bed beside me. Although the scene was like old times, the feelings weren't there anymore. We watched a second movie, other than his leg touching mine, we didn't touch at all.

"I better go, it's getting late."

"Alright, let me walk you downstairs." After Sterling unlocked the door, I gave him a one arm hug and said goodbye. I was proud of myself because I did not have a desire to sleep with him or even kiss him.

Over the next several weeks, Sterling and I kept in contact. Our conversations were very casual. We talked about everything that didn't pertain to us directly. Finally, the topic of our next sexual encounter arose when he asked when were going to do it again.

"Sterling, I am cool on you, there will not be a next time. You can't have none no more, I am so over you." That is when the altar male ego arose.

"You know you wanted me to do it to you that night you came over and watched movies."

"No dear I didn't, believe me if I did, you would have gave me some." I don't know why he thought I couldn't resist him. I enjoyed getting to know Sterling outside of the bedroom. We were talking almost daily; I was happy that we learned to be friends. I was able to be around Sterling and not have my emotions aroused. Just when you think you are firmly planted to what you believe a curve ball comes your way to test the theory.

I needed an escort for this network event and Lawson did not want to go. I didn't see the harm in inviting Sterling to escort me. This event would give him the opportunity to network. I gave him all the particulars of what to wear, the place, and time. We decided that we would ride together, and I would pick him up. I really didn't anticipate him to follow through. I was surprised when I received a text message from him asking what time was I planning to pick him up. He was infamous for being a no call, no show. If I thought he was going to really go, I would have gotten cuter, but the yellow ¾ length linen jacket and wide leg white linen pants would have to work today.

When I arrived to pick up Sterling, his roommate let me know that he was on his way downstairs. I introduced myself to his roommate and engaged in small talk. Sterling came down the stairs. I was breathless. He was in a navy-blue suit, gray shirt, blue and gray tie, cuff links and the whole nine yards. You talk about booted and suited; He looked like DAMN! I was taken back. I could not establish direct eye contact with Sterling. I was having flashbacks of the first time I saw him in a suit and what happened then. I wanted to mail my check to the charity and network upstairs.

As we rode to the event, we engaged in idle chatter. I for one was thinking up stuff to say other than,

"Can we go do it right now?" I went as far as showing him photos of my children that was in my wallet. We talked about traffic, current events, and the music that was playing softly in the background. It was hard for me to focus, Sterling was wearing his *come get me cologne*. I was so happy when we finally made it to the convention center because I don't know how much longer I would have been able to sit next to him and keep my hands to myself.

Arriving at the venue, Sterling checked in and got his name badge. We entered the banquet room; I thought we should start the evening off with a quick drink. Sterling escorted me to the bar and ordered wine for us both. I greeted colleagues, Sterling networked. I made sure it didn't look like we were on a date or together for that fact of the matter. I didn't want him to feel like I was babysitting him. Ok I am lying; I was trying to keep my distance because kitty was purring. I was ready to just put my thoughts out there.

Sterling made it extremely difficult for me to keep the purpose of the evening and our relationship in perceptive. Every time I managed to blend into the crowd he found me, checking to see if I wanted a drink or a bite to eat. He consistently tried to feed me because up to this point, I had not stopped long enough to make a plate. Sterling was attentive and a gentlemen. When he talked to me, he held the small of my back and spoke close to my ear. When he leaned in to speak to me, I shivered inside. My imagination of what the evening had in store ran wild. I still could not make direct eye contact because I would have been mesmerized and completely submissive to whatever he willed. I was grateful Sterling didn't know how to read me, if so; he would have known I would have gotten undressed for him with a simple wink of his eye.

Sterling behaved as if we were the room's power couple. He worked the room with comfort and ease. He was polite, professional, and observant. Sterling convinced me that I should have some food. While standing in the buffet line, Sterling leaned extremely close to my face,

"Oh, I am sorry about the frontal." He said. I didn't respond.

"I said sorry about the frontal, I guess that just went over your head. I just leaned in front of you." Sterling repeated. Apparently, he must have forgotten who he was dealing with, so it was my responsibility to remind him.

"I need you to quit playing. Remember the last time you got that close to me in a suit, I did it to you in your office." I said softly. He smiled and looked at the server.

"I wonder how much of that she heard, but that's right, huh? We did do it in my office, I forgot about that." He said sarcastically. See he was not playing fair. He was trying really hard to make me handle him. But I was playing it cool.

"Sterling, I am not giving you no booty." I insisted as I stepped away from the buffet. He rolled his eyes at me and said,

"You don't have to keep reminding me." Little did he know I wasn't reminding him; I was trying to convince myself.

Sterling finally ran into a couple of gentlemen that he knew. When he greeted them, he didn't introduce me. At first, I was little bothered by the fact he hadn't made an introduction, but I remembered women are courteous and men are needful. If he didn't introduce them to me that meant they weren't worth me knowing. I tried to casually slip into the crowd to allow them to have there guy talk, but when I turned away, Sterling began to eat off my plate. I thought it was cute, he was making it known that I was with him. The way he made his presence known intrigued me. It's funny how men always mark their territory just like a dog.

The fashion show started. Sterling and I found a place close to the runway. We were worse than two little kids. We critiqued the model's attire. Sterling was resting his head against mine whispering about the corny outfits that the men were modeling. As an attempt to get him under control before I fell on the ground in laughter I said,

"If you don't stop, I will buy you that outfit right there, the one the guy is walking out in now." Sterling looked up to see a man coming down the runway in green and brown polka dot and checkered outfit.

"Oh hell naw! That is just plain ugly." He exclaimed.

"I think it is cute, I like it." I responded. A gentleman standing behind us overheard our conversation and interjected,

"I like it too; it's cool you know abstract." Sterling turned to the guy and said,

"Abstract is a nice way of saying something is ugly as hell. That outfit is so ugly that it could be cool. Fools will give you cool points for having the courage to wear that. They will look at you to say you actually dressed like that on purpose and came outside." We all just laughed.

The evening was winding down; I was not ready for my evening with Sterling to end.

"Do you have time for us to stop by my house before I drop you off?" I asked.

"Sure, one of my boys is coming by to watch the game, but I got some time." I have known Sterling for more than seven years and in all that time he has never known where I lived. He was surprised when I made the suggestion. The ride to my place was a little awkward.

"Did you enjoy yourself?"

"Yeah, I made some cool contacts I noticed the people in the buffet line were friendlier than the small groups of people that were huddled together. There was no way to step into one of the circles."

I gave him the nickel tour of my house and he spoke to my children. We ended the tour in my workroom.

"Let me show you something." I showed him the encyclopedia of songs that I had written.

"Feel free to browse and read whatever. I'll be back; I'm going to get out these clothes." Returning to my workroom, Sterling was sitting reading my songs with a smile on his face.

"You wrote these?"

"Yes, sir."

"Wow, do you plan to sell them? Damn girl they are good."

"I think after I copyright them, I will try to sell them, I don't know though because these are my most intimate thoughts."

Sterling's friend called while he was reading.

"Go ahead over man; I am on my way to the crib in a minute." Sterling said to his friend on the phone. After he hung up I said,

"Well, let me take you home."

"Give me a second; I want to finish reading this last one." He responded.

"The one you are reading now I wrote about you." I said with a smile. Sterling read the lyrics,

"Wow this is really about us. Baby, you are talented. Thank you for sharing them with me." He was surprised that I was able to capture the memories of our relationship into words.

"I am surprised you remember all this and it reads like a story." Sterling said with a light chuckle.

Sterling only lived a couple of minutes away from me. During the ride, we talked about Pete and Auntie Gwen.

"You know it was Auntie Gwen that told me that you bought a house with that girl, she said that you were talking about it in front of her knowing she was my aunt and would tell me. She thought you wanted me to stop you.

"What is Auntie Gwen doing these days?"

"She is back in Indiana now, but she is doing fine." Sterling did a great job evading the conversation by changing the subject. Naked, Sterling and I could talk about anything, but it seemed like we worked to avoid intimacy since we weren't having sex anymore.

I hoped for a goodnight kiss because I would take that opportunity to get some. I know Sterling would give me some whenever I asked so I have no idea why I didn't have the courage to ask for what I wanted. Before getting out of my truck, Sterling leaned over and kissed me on the cheek.

"Thanks, I had a great time. I will call you tomorrow. Bye." That was a bittersweet goodbye. His kiss was so sweet and endearing, but at the same time, I was not ready to say goodbye. It's been years since he and I slept together, and I was ripe for the picking. Throughout the night, Sterling and I text messaged each other. I had to break it down. *Ok, that suit did it for me. If I would have known that I wouldn't have left. Well the children were home so I would have behaved. Oh, so it was fake? No, it was very real, just under control.*

Things between Sterling and I looked to be going in the right direction. I still hadn't told him about Lawson. I guess because I did not know where things stood between me and Lawson. I found a reason to see Sterling at least once a week. I enjoyed being in his presence because he was so comforting and encouraging. I missed being intimate with him. Sterling had the opportunity to see me in a new light, would he consider us being a couple now. I called Sterling to see how his job hunting was going.

"What's up baby, I got drunk last night, and I got an interview in a couple of hours, I'm hurting bad."

"Oh, the baby is hung over?"

"I am a HAM. A Hot Ass Mess! I want to do it and go to sleep." He is always throwing these small hints of seduction at me. I always tried to evade them with a play on words. I knew good and hell well what he was saying but I played it off.

"Do the interview, then go home and go to bed."

"No, I want to do it, and then go to sleep." He repeated.

"Can you leave? Baby why don't you come by?"

"No, I just got back from lunch."

Imagination will get you caught up every time. Our sexual hiatus did not negate desire.

"I'm gonna put on my favorite suit. It's brown with my blue shirt; it has the white cuffs and collars. I got on my gold cuff links, and a matching blue and brown tie. I am gonna throw on my chocolate gators." Sterling spoke seductively. The visual alone was turning me on, then to couple that with his voice. He was using his bedroom voice at 1 o'clock in the afternoon. I was ready to walk out the office. Before I could reply, he continued,

"Why don't you leave the office and come over. I am laying here thinking about making love to you. I can taste your pussy on my mouth, and your juices running down my chin. I got it out picturing you riding it."

This was not fair! I wanted to leave the office and handle that for him. I got up and shut my office door.

"Sterling I need you to quit talking to me like that."

"Come over, it's ready for you."

"Baby you need to put that away and get up. If I come over there you will not make it to your interview because I will let you lick me from asshole to appetite. I will let you smack it from the back, and then just for old time's sake, I will swallow. You know after that you will not be good for nothing but a nap. I really need you to stop."

The na na was talking to me, but I knew I had to say no. Sterling thought differently.

"I am laying here holding it, stroking it, remembering how you used to move up and down on it." I knew I couldn't leave, but I felt it was my civic duty to handle that for him, you know, walk him to his climax. I rested my head in my hand and began to speak.

"Daddy, you remember momma sitting on it, moving quickly on the tip, while you palmed my ass." I moaned.

"Daddy I can feel your lips moving down my cheek, kissing my neck, nibbling across my shoulder as you massaged every part of my body, finally sliding your fingers between my legs. Remember how soft and wet I am, remember how good I taste, think of the harmonic sounds when we made love." I emulated the sounds and within seconds from the other end of the phone, I heard the finale.

"Yes baby yes, I'm cumming deep inside of you." Sterling yelled. He had came now what in the hell was I supposed to do?

"Daddy, feel better now?"

"Yes, good looking out thanks. Let me go clean up and I will holla back later." That let me know that I did the right thing by not going over there because I might have only got 3 strokes out the deal and had to come back to work hot and bothered for real.

"Hey, can I stop by; I am just leaving the barber."

"Sure, come on through, I am just laying here." When I walked into Sterling's place, he was laid out on the couch loosely covered with nothing but a blanket. Damn, I hate it when he doesn't play fair! I am a sucker for broad shoulders and a nice chest. I could have acted out what I talked him through over the phone. Sterling's face lit up like Christmas as he looked at what I called his "big boy" prizes in the bag I handed him. I sat on his lap as he looked at his gifts.

"Thank you, baby, you are so sweet to me." I got up to leave and Sterling grabbed me by the back of my pants and smiled. He was making it more and more difficult to resist his advances.

"Sterling, I wish you would get yourself together, quit being scary and act right so we can get married, that way we can do it twice a day everyday, that in itself should be an incentive for you to get it together." I said with a smile as I headed towards the door.

"Actually, it is." He whispered,

"Love you bye."

"Love you too baby."

Sterling was on my mind constantly, he was engrained in my heart. Pretending I had no romantic interest in him was very difficult for me. I know he loves me but what was the hang up? I made sure I called and checked on him every few days.

"So how are you sir? Are you alright?"

"I'm good, I'm always alright?"

"Is there anything that I can do?"

"The one thing that you can do, you aren't willing to do, so I'm cool."

"I keep telling you there is more to me than what you get when I gap my legs open. My best attributes are outside the bedroom."

"Baby, I'm just fine."

"You are gonna miss me when I'm gone."

"I sure will, but why would you want to leave me alone?"

"Sterling, I don't want to but I am tired of wanting someone who doesn't want me. One day I'm gonna quit you for real." I have to admit, I felt hurt that he only thought of me as a piece of ass. But what could I do? This dance was starting to get old. I am ready for a new beat.

Chapter XV

Men suck, I was done for real. Between Lawson and Sterling, I promise I will never love again. At this point, I don't care if I ever have sex again. To ensure that falling in love was not an option for me, I filled my life with activity to satisfy the gaps of not being in a relationship. I became team mom, adult mentor, committee member, and volunteer. It seemed like I spent all of my meeting, coming and going. One Thursday evening my daughter thought it was nice to let me know that she volunteered me to cook a pot of greens and macaroni and cheese for the Ebony Club Potluck the next day. I took off work the next day in order to get everything prepared.

Two of my children were on program, which meant I had to be there early and help set up. I just love my kids; I was also volunteered to help serve the buffet line as well. I greeted the parents and replenished the food when I noticed a gentleman that I did not know come through the line. He was very attractive that meant he was worth more trouble than I was willing to endure.

"Excuse me, who made these greens? They are screaming."

"I made them, thank you."

"I am ashamed of myself; this is my second trip up here. I was not expecting food like this. I thought we were gonna get food thrown together by the cafeteria." When I didn't reply, the stranger walked away.

Ebony Club's sponsoring teacher introduced the keynote speaker of the evening as Mr. Trevor Evans. The stranger from the buffet line was the speaker of the evening. If I would have known who he was, I would have been a little nicer. Trevor gave a great motivational message for the children. I found his talk interesting, but I was drafted into the cleanup crew, so I did not get to hear his whole message or see him anymore that evening.

Chicago was in town to play a basketball game; I took the children to see the game as an outing. We ran into Trevor. Trevor and I seemed to run into each other at least once a week. I thought this was interesting because up to this point, I never seen him and now he is everywhere I am.

"If I keep running into you like this, I am going to begin to think you are stalking me." I said.

"To make sure you don't call the police on me for stalking you, you can just invite me to go with you."

"Sounds like a winner." We exchanged business cards, I never heard from him.

My son was preparing for college and was looking into a few organizations for scholarships and volunteer opportunities. I was watching the evening news and Trevor was being honored because of his contribution to the community as a volunteer and motivational speaker. I thought he would be a great resource for direction for my son. I called Trevor a few times without a return call. Just as I thought, he was like every other man in Denver, he lacked personal integrity. He could not return a simple phone call.

It was that time for my annual youth charity dinner and this year I was on program. During the meet and greet, Trevor surfaced, I spoke to him in passing. After the presentations, Trevor found his way to me.

"Sheridyn, I didn't know that you were involved with the youth charity organization?"

"Yes I have volunteered with the organization for several years, and assumed a board position last year." I really did not have much to say to him because I felt it was a waste of time.

"I know you called me a couple of times; I am so sorry I haven't returned your call."

"Trevor I learned a long time ago that if people deem something as insignificant, it receives low priority and no attention. So are you sorry for thinking I am insignificant?"

"Sheridyn, it is not like that, I have just been busy."

"Exactly, thank you for proving my point because you thought I was insignificant, returning my call was not a priority." I smiled at him and turned to greet other people in the room. I was not about to start wasting my time with someone who thought I was insignificant.

One morning, I decided to run before heading to the office. I heard a man's voice yell.

"Quick, somebody dial 911, this woman is stalking me." It was Trevor, sitting in the grass stretching.

"You know my kids go to this school; you have probably been camping out here everyday since I met you, hoping you would see me dropping them off for school."

"Hell, the last time I saw you, you chewed a brother up and spit him out."

"The truth is still the truth whether you choose to accept it or not. Sorry if I bruised your ego."

"Will you cut me some slack? Can you be friendly for just a minute?"

"I am always friendly, just honest."

"So are you finishing up or starting off?" I asked.

"I was just about to get started, wanna run together?"

"Sure." Our run was great; Trevor and I talked like we were old friends. This time, we even set a date. Trevor wanted the opportunity to change my opinion of him.

Trevor was a great guy; I was waiting to find out what was wrong with him. When was the wife, six kids, prison record, or drug habit going to surface? Surprisingly, he was all that he presented himself to be. The next several months, he was a dream come true. Trevor created a place for himself in my life. He was at my daughter's track meets and my son's football games. He even made it a point to come to their awards ceremonies.

Trevor took me downtown for the evening. The weather was perfect. It was warm, mild, and breezy. We walked around, held hands, listened to live music, and sat on the patio of a restaurant for appetizers and drinks. We laughed and talked, but as soon as we were quiet for more than two minutes, I found myself thinking about Sterling wishing I was with him.

"What are you thinking about?" Trevor asked.

"Nothing, I'm just enjoying the scenery and soaking in the atmosphere," I responded. There was no politically correct way to say I wish you were someone else. I opted to do what any lady in my position would do; I leaned in and kissed Trevor.

"Thank you for a perfect evening." I lied but it was better than the truth.

Things between Trevor and I began to perk up. We were laughing, having fun, and experiencing new things together. Without realizing it, I have not thought about Sterling in close to a year. Things with Trevor and I progressed, we were growing to love each other. During dinner one evening, Trevor proposed to me. I was so surprised because up to this point, we had never even discussed marriage. I said yes. I was excited that I was getting married; I didn't know who to tell first.

The next morning, I stopped by my mother's beauty shop to share the news. Ms. Shirley was there.

"Baby, you don't look like you are excited to be getting married." Ms. Shirley said, looking over the top of her glasses at the ring.

"Ms. Shirley I am elated. I am marrying a man named Trevor, and yes, he loves me." Ms. Shirley lifted up the hair dyer and asked,

"My question is do you love him?"

"Yes, ma'am I do."

"I hear what your mouth is saying, but I also see your heart. That other guy still has your heart bound." Old people can always see through any masquerade. I guess I had to come clean.

"Trevor doesn't make me feel like Sterling does, but I know Trevor is who I need in my life. He is good for me and the kids." Ms. Shirley signaled for me to come sit beside her.

"Baby, love is not a look or feeling, love is a verb, love is an action word. That is all I have to say."

Ms. Shirley is always dropping heavy nuggets on a sistah when I ain't prepared. I think my mother was so happy that I was finally getting married that she could care less who I was marrying. I can't deny what I was feeling. I think I needed to make sure there was not a chance that Sterling and I would be together before I started planning my wedding with Trevor.

I had my fill of Sterling's uncertainty. I had to see what was up with us before moving forward. I asked Sterling if we could go on a date this coming weekend. He was more than excited about seeing the movie. We made plans to get together on Friday. You guessed it, Sterling was a no call, no show. Once again, I was disappointed although I wasn't surprised.

During a conversation that Sterling and I had before, he said I never made my intentions known to him. I decided to put myself out there. I sent Sterling an email. *Are you gonna be my boyfriend or what?* Sterling didn't acknowledge the email. The fact that he didn't reply bothered me. Why did he want me to stay in limbo? He didn't want me, but he wouldn't want to let me go either. That is what made dealing with him so hard.

I was home alone one evening and I thought I would call Sterling to see if he wanted to join me for dinner. Before I could ask to invite him to dinner, he told me that he was headed to a friend's party and didn't want to. I had to ask.

"Whose party is it?"

"This one dude we call Red. You don't know how bad I just want to stay in bed."

"Why are you going to the party if you don't feel like it? People should be used to you not showing up."

"I know but this fool's feelings will be all hurt if I don't show up so I gotta go." That did it for me. This Red wasn't one of his closest friends because I knew all of them. He was more concerned about his boy's feelings and not disappointing him than he had ever been about mine. What Ms. Shirley said finally made sense to me. It was time for me to walk away.

"Madison, I have fooled around and got caught up with Sterling again and as usual, he got me chasing my tail."

"Girl, let me tell you, Sterling is not gonna ever commit to you, because he can't imagine you ever being with anyone else. You have given him the impression that you are his forever and as long as he believes that he got you, nothing will change. Men are hunters and once they conquer, they lose interest. I know you love Sterling, you know I am rooting for him, but it is time you face the truth and move on."

I was tired of being confused and unsure. I knew what I had to do but it was so hard. It sounds crazy but holding on was easier than letting go, but I had to find the courage to move on. I called Sterling and asked if he could give me $20. I made up a story that I had left my ATM card in my other purse. I didn't need the money, but it was an excuse to see him. Of course, Sterling told me to come over and get it. We stood in the kitchen and talked for 10 minutes about nothing. I was building up the courage to kiss him, because I knew this kiss would be goodbye forever. Sterling started drinking a beer. I took a deep breath and asked,

"Can I kiss you before I leave?" Sterling looked at me with a smile and said,

"Of course, you can but I just finished drinking a beer." I smiled and replied,

"I have kissed you while your mouth has tasted like other things like food, liquor, and me!" Sterling leaned in to kiss me and said,

"That is what I was looking for you to say, I like kissing you with you on my mouth." We began to kiss subtle and soft. We embraced each other; we started to get a little carried away with the kiss and started touching each other underneath our clothes. I stopped him before he got too intimate.

"Why are you afraid to love me? Since, the night that we met, you have known that I had more to offer you than an orgasm."

"I have never led you on; I have always been honest with you. You have always been there for me, and I love you for that." I couldn't believe what I was hearing.

"Sheridyn, I enjoy hanging with you, you are the sweetest woman that I know, and the sex is off the hook, you are my girl, but I'm just not feeling you like that." My soul hurt to hear him say that." I managed to hold back the tears.

"Thank you for being honest with me." I said with a smile as I headed out the door.

I had been sidetracked for over a week. It was time to get focused. I was scheduled to get married in a few months and I had not made any plans. I hadn't even called my family and friends outside of Colorado yet. It was time for me to move full steam ahead. The first call I made was to Madison.

"I was wondering if you are doing anything on June 20th?"

"Girl, are you saying what I think you are saying? Are you getting married?"

"Yes ma'am."

"Congratulations, you didn't tell me Sterling finally got it together."

"He didn't, I am marrying Trevor." Madison was silent for a moment.

"Are you sure you want to marry him? I'm just saying, I don't think you love him; you just love things about him." I know that Madison has my best interest at heart, but I need my friend to be happy for me right now.

"Girl, Trevor really loves me, although we don't laugh or have wild unbridled sex like I did with Sterling, I know Trevor will protect me and love me unconditionally. I know if I died tomorrow, receiving an insurance check would sadden him. For those reasons, I said yes."

"Sheridyn, I know you are ready to get married, I know Trevor is a good man, but I don't think he is the right man for you."

"Really, based upon what? You have never met Trevor."

"Sheridyn, I know you. I have seen you in love, I have listened to you talk about Trevor and it doesn't sound the same. You don't talk about him the way you talked about Sterling. You know you are my girl, and you know I will be in Colorado with bells on. I just want to make sure you aren't making a mistake. You have waited this long to get married; I would hate to see you marry the wrong person."

"I know that if I died tomorrow my children will be well taken care of."

"But what if you live another 50 years? Will 50 years with him be a life or a life sentence?"

"Madison it is really important that you are here to share my special day with me, but if you are going to be negative about the situation, I will find someone else to be my maid of honor."

"Sheri, yes, I called you Sheri like yo momma calls you to quit tripping, I got your back. You just give me the particulars, by the way, congratulations stinky!" We laughed.

"Ok, I know you got other friends and stuff, but I am pulling rank. I am in charge of the bachelorette party."

"It's all you. I will holla back later."

Trevor and I decided that we would not have sex until our honeymoon, but I woke up with the na na on fire! I had relations with myself twice that still did not quench the fire burning deep inside. Crossing my legs even made me wet. I finally broke down and sent Sterling a text. *Can I do it to you later? Of course? When? After 9. I am free before 9. Oh well never mind. Call me after 9 then. Alright.*

I called Sterling after 9, he was at the club and I needed to go pick him up. I arrived at the club; he had my Goose on the rocks waiting for me. I greeted all of his homeboys, I took a seat and Sterling joined me. After I finished my drink, we headed out. On the way to my truck, Sterling stopped to hit the blunt at his boy's car. I was mad about it, Sterling know he can't handle smoking and drinking. After all this, I knew I was about to get some raggedy dick. Damn!

Sterling and I talked casually as we headed down the highway; he began to rub my chest.

"You don't know nothing about that."

"Yes I do, that is a padded, push up bruh." Sterling said as he moved his hand underneath my bra and started sucking my nipple. It felt so good.

"You better stop before I pull over. We won't make it to your house." He acted like I didn't say a word.

Arriving at Sterling's place, we didn't even turn on the lights; I stepped to him and began kissing him. I took his cell phone and keys out of his hand and put his hands on my ass. He palmed my ass and I nibbled on his chest. Sterling grabbed me by the face sliding his fingers through my hair and began to kiss me with great passion. I pulled his shirt off and unhooked my bra.

Sterling pulled off my pants and my thong. He bent me over the arm of the black leather sofa as he got on his knees. He started eating me from behind. I began to get wetter and moan in elation and he spread my cheeks apart and licked me more diligently. I remembered we were in the middle of his living room floor,

"Not to break the mood, but we need to move this behind a closed door, what if your roommate walks in?"

"He won't be home tonight, Sterling said as he flipped me onto my back.

All I felt was Sterling's soft tongue waver between my lips and across my clit as he slid his fingers inside of me. I was in awe; calmness came over me as I slowly released the best orgasm I have ever had in my life. I came so hard, that my stomach muscles tightened. I was ready to feel him inside of me. I pushed him off me and unbuckled his pants. As his pants hit the floor, with nothing but my mouth, I grabbed him by the tip of his erection and deep throated him, he ran his fingers through my hair.

"That feels so good, but not yet." Sterling said as he pushed me away from him. I sat him on the sofa; I placed him inside of me. I squeezed tightly as he stroked deeper and deeper.

Riding Sterling, with my back to him, he grabbed my breasts as if he was kneading dough. With a deep sigh, he said,

"Let's take this upstairs." I walked towards the stairs in front of him, after climbing a few steps, I bent over and hiked my ass high in the air, Sterling moved right in. I bounced my ass and he palmed it like a basketball. I moved forward so that he would slide out. I walked to the top of the stairs and laid on my back. Sterling grabbed the back of my thigh and pushed it upward as he stuck himself inside of me. I only let him get a couple of strokes before I moved further up the stairs. I got up and began to walk to his bedroom.

Sterling threw his clothes off the bed and laid on the bed and said,

"Come here." On my hands and knees, I started crawling across the bed to him.

"No, I said come here. I want to taste you first." He said forcefully as he grabbed me under my arms and pulled me onto his mouth. Sterling gripped my ass as he licked me and sucked me gently. Then, Sterling grabbed my hair and pulled my head backwards. With a steep arch in my back, I continued riding his face. I released the best orgasm known to mankind,

"Keep cumming baby I want all of it. You taste good as hell." I inhaled and finally broke away from him.

I slid down his body until I was on top of his dick, I pushed him inside of me and I laid on him. The tango began; I was riding him, kissing him, and licking my juices from around his mouth and sucking his tongue. I firmly nibbled on Sterling's nipples and he began to pull my hair and moan, we were in sync.

"I am not ready to cum." Sterling whispered as he rolled me onto my back. Sterling grabbed both of my legs and pushed them towards the headboard. He began to hit it with authority and pride. I was ready to throw in the towel and cry uncle so I whispered,

"I am ready to stop for a minute."

"Hell naw, I have waited too long for this, I am gonna get it all. I will let you rest for a minute."

Sterling let my legs down and he laid still inside of me. He literally only let me rest for 60 seconds before he started moving again. I wasn't gonna let him get the best of me, so I flipped my leg over his head to let him get it from the side. That turned him on.

"Damn, girl you are gonna make me cum." After just a couple of strokes to build up the passion, I rolled onto my stomach and arched my back. Hiking my ass high into the air, I controlled the movement. I used my thigh muscles to move so that I could make my ass shake vigorously.

"Damn girl, baby stop." Sterling uttered as he smacked my ass. He pulled out. "I am not ready to cum yet."

With my ass still tooted up in the air, I began to touch myself and fondle Sterling. He pulled me by the arm and started sucking my juices off my fingers.

"Girl, you are so wet."

"You want to be inside of me?"

"Yes."

"Put it back in." As soon as Sterling got back inside of me, I moved my ass up, down, and in small circles. That drove Sterling wild. He moaned loudly, and screamed in ecstasy.

"Baby roll over on your back, damn girl, I miss you, baby I miss this." Once I was on my back, Sterling gave it to me purposefully and passionately. I raised my pelvis off the bed and began to throw it back at him.

"Damn, girl."

"Daddy like it? It is wet enough? Is daddy ready to cum inside his pussy?" I seductively whispered.

"Yes, damn girl, I can't hold it I am cumming." Sterling shouted as he hit the bottom to release.

Sterling came, and then he laid his head on my stomach and went to sleep. After a few moments, I tried to move. He said, no and went back to sleep. Eventfully, I fell asleep, but not for long because Sterling was lying on my stomach between my legs and that was not comfortable. I guess he forgot he weighs 250 pounds. I managed to get from underneath him; I finally got comfortable and went to sleep.

I woke up at the crack of dawn; everything on my body was sore. I didn't wake Sterling, when I got out the bed. I got dressed and left. Later that evening, Sterling sent me a text *thanks that was great when can we do it again? It was the best sex I ever had but it will not happen again. Sterling, I realized that I used to love you, but over time, I stopped loving you. But I continued to hold on not because I wanted to be with you, but because I was afraid to love anyone else. Thanks for last night, now I am free to love.* I replied.

It was the strangest thing, I felt relieved, whatever I released when I had sex with Sterling freed me. I was ready to marry Trevor; I knew that I was marrying the right man without any regrets. I didn't feel guilt about my moment of indiscretion because it felt like a necessary catalyst. I was glad that I had the opportunity to get with Sterling one last time. I believe this time; he is out of my system for real. Sterling periodically texted me, but I took it for what it was, idol banter.

I was anxious and overwhelmed with pulling together a perfect wedding in less than six months. But I was bound and determined to make my special day great. I was proud to become Mrs. Trevor Evans. I can honestly say that I loved Trevor and I was ready to give him my all. Trevor treated me like a princess. Most importantly, he loved me even more than I loved him. He knew what excited me and took a genuine interest in the things that was important to me.

I thought my calendar was cluttered; Trevor was more of a socialite than I was. He held several board positions which meant that we were consistently meeting, entertaining, and being entertained, but somehow, he always found the time to shower me with attention and affection. Whether it was waking me up with Starbucks in the morning or surprising me on a business trip, Trevor made sure he expressed how much he loved me. I hate to admit it, but some days, I didn't think I deserved him. I asked God what did I do to be blessed with such a man. He was a provider, a protector, strong and yet tender.

Trevor owned his own company and had been working hard for weeks, trying to close a few deals and tied up loose ends before the wedding process began. We made it a point to see each other everyday because we weren't living together yet. We were scheduled to move into our house about a week or so after the wedding. Trevor was working 14-hour days, six days a week, and eating on the run. Although we talked several times a day, I had not seen Trevor in almost a week.

I decided that I would surprise Trevor at his office. I was missing him. I let myself into his office. Trevor was sitting behind his desk with his tie loosened, sipping a watered-down cola, and comparing spreadsheets. He had his jazz playing softly. Trevor was so engulfed in what he was doing, that he didn't even notice that I walked in. I watched him work for a few seconds.

"If I write numbers on me, could I have some attention too?" I asked. Trevor stood up from his desk and looked at me with the biggest smile.

"If you had numbers on you, you would have my attention." He began to walk towards me, "but since you don't have numbers on you, you have my love, my affection, and my soul, not just my attention." Trevor said before he kissed me.

"You keep this up; I might ask you to marry me." I said.

"What are you doing here sweetheart?"

"I know that you are working hard, so I thought I would bring you something to nibble on, oh yeah, and something for dinner too."

"I am the luckiest man alive, thank you for agreeing to marry me. I look forward to dinner with you every night." I unpacked the picnic basket of food I had prepared.

"What are you working on, do you need some help?"

"I am putting together a proposal for a government bid. I am still trying to pull together the numbers. Other than that, I got it under control. But, once I get it all together, I would like you to help me organize it."

"I would be delighted to help."

I enjoyed being with Trevor, he was practical, romantic, and he valued me. Here we were sitting in the middle of his office floor having dinner, and Trevor began to rub my feet. It's amazing that it was that moment that I saw Trevor for the first time. I never really recognized him or how much joy he brought to my life until that moment.

Chapter XVI

The day that I dreamed of since I was a little girl had finally arrived, my wedding day. I was nervously excited that my day had finally come. Trevor was the perfect man, and this day was going to be perfect. Sitting in my dressing room at the church, Madison fussed with my hair. Naomi walked through the church like a drill sergeant performing a final walk through; checking to make sure everything was running like clockwork. I was proud of the work Naomi had done in preparation for this day.

Naomi, Sabrina, Madison and I all used to work together. Naomi was a flower child trapped in the body of a Type-A personality. Naomi wore her hair natural and marched to the beat of her own drum. She thought the world should be filled with rainbows, puppy dogs and ice cream cones. She thought dressing appropriately for brunch was considered conformity. What made her interesting was when it came to the things she was concerned about or that she controlled, she managed to the letter with an iron fist.

As my wedding coordinator, Naomi made sure that all I had to do on my wedding day was show up and get married. She had offended some of the wedding party, but she was doing exactly what she was hired to which was to keep this day *stress free*. Naomi was polite and professional but had a no-nonsense approach when she was focused on a task.

"Sheridyn, the flowers have arrived, they look absolutely wonderful. Everything is in its place, and everyone is present and accounted for. We just need you front and center, then we can get this party started." Naomi said as she walked back into my dressing room. Just as she completed her sentence, we heard a faint knock on the door. Naomi opened the door.

"Hi, I'm here to see Sheridyn." The voice from the door was familiar, but I didn't look up because I knew Naomi would handle whoever it was.

"Sir, the bride is preparing to get married. She will have time to talk to you during the reception, now goodbye."

Madison had an animated grin on her face. When I looked up to see what she was so excited about, I saw Sterling's reflection in the mirror, he was dressed in a tuxedo standing at the door. Madison was not only smiling, but she was silently clapping her hands. Had she arranged this? Did she have Sterling show up to sabotage my day? I hoped Madison would not betray me like this.

"I need to talk to you; can you please ask everyone to leave?" Sterling whispered. Naomi wasn't having it.

"Excuse me, what did I just say? The bride is about to get married, as her wedding coordinator, it's my job to see this day goes off without a hitch, and you sir would be defined as a major hitch. You will have to talk to her at the reception." Naomi said adamantly as she grabbed him by the arm and tried to lead him out the door.

"No, Naomi its ok. Could everyone step out and give us a couple of minutes?" I asked. Naomi looked at me as if I had three heads.

"I'm glad I added in 10 minutes of wiggle room. He got 7 minutes, then his ass gotta get the hell outta here!" Naomi exclaimed. Once everyone left the room, Sterling slowly walked over to me and knelt down on one knee.

"Sheridyn, you look absolutely beautiful. You look like heaven. I love you and I'm here to tell you, that you are making a mistake. You are marrying the wrong man. That man can't possibly love you like I do. I know you don't have the magic with him that we shared. I have been stupid. I have always loved you. I was afraid of loving someone as much as I love you. We always seemed to vibe and our rhythm was great. I came here today to tell you that I love you and I want to marry you. Will you be my wife?"

Tears streamed down my face. Sterling wrapped his arms around me, laid his head on my abdomen and held me tightly. My eyes began to fill with tears.

"In real life girl, I love you and the thought of not having you in my life is killing me." Sterling stood up and gently wiped the tears from my face.

"So will you do me the honor of being my rib?" I closed my eyes and sighed heavily.

"Sterling, you don't know how long I waited for this day to come? To hear you say that you want me as your wife, it is sweet music to my ears. I used to fantasize about how I thought you would propose to me. I dreamed about all the fun we would have at the reception. I imagined how electric our honeymoon would be. I even imagined sharing the rest of our lives together. Having you as a husband would be any woman's fantasy." I whispered.

"Let me ask you this, how did you know I was getting married today?"

"It was fate. My barber was sick, and I needed to get my fade tightened up. I decided to let one of the other barbers touch me up. He told me that I was his last head for the day because one of his customers was getting married. When he handed me the invitation, I saw that his client was marrying you. As soon as he finished, I got changed and came straight over here." Sterling replied. I closed my eyes and inhaled deeply and stepped out of Sterling's arms.

"For years, I anticipated you professing your love to me and us living happily ever after. I would be honored to be your wife. Pete once told me all men have that one great love they let get away and I was that great love that you let get away." Before I could continue Sterling interrupted,

"Pete knew what he was talking about. I love you. I took your love for granted." I shook my head no.

"What Pete was telling me is that you decided way back then that you were not gonna be with me. Sterling, I can't marry you, sometimes rhythm can't keep time and love just ain't enough. I have moved on. It means a lot to me that you are here right now because I needed the closure, but I am about to marry a man that is in love with me. My smile is what he lives for. He has pledged to me that he would make sure that I have a smile on my face for the rest of my life. I know 20 years from now, your stomach will hurt because you let me go, but you don't want to marry me. You just want to win. You want me in your life." I continued.

"Sheridyn, how many times have you said that you were leaving me alone, but didn't? Baby, let's just do this you know you want me as much as I want you."

"Sterling you already walked away from me. Have you told Tajuana that it was over, or does she still believe that you are going to marry her in a couple of hours? This would be different if you just heard I was getting married and came to stop me. If you don't want to marry her, then don't. But don't use me as a scapegoat. Now that I have experienced true love, I know what we had was just lust." I responded.

"I know you still love me because of the night we shared a few months ago."

"I was horny that is why that night a few months ago happened."

"Sheridyn, how can you say that? What we share is so special. Look at me and tell me you don't love me."

"The issue isn't me loving you; the issue is you, and the fact that you don't really love me. You love the fact that I love you. You love what I represent. You love me so much that you are marrying someone else." I answered.

"Well, I wanted to see what was up with us before I broke things off with her. I don't want to break her heart for no reason."

I was confused and dumbfounded. I could not believe what I was hearing. I guess it is time for me to call Sterling out and let him know how I knew he is scheduled to marry another woman today. Until this moment, I have never held Sterling accountable for hurting me. Rather than holding him accountable, I lowered my expectations of him. I dismissed Sterling for not keeping his word because I loved him, and I felt I didn't have the right to say anything about what he had with other people. After all, we weren't exclusive. This was typical Sterling though, to not acknowledge what he had done or was doing was wrong. I don't think the words I'm sorry exist in his vocabulary.

"Sterling, once again, you love her so much that you want to save her heartache. That is love, heartaches and orgasms are not love. That is all you've ever given me." I stated.

"Sterling listen to yourself, you are treating love as if it was an algebra equation *if* things work out the way I intend *then* I will follow my heart. Life and definitely love does not have an, *if and then or when* clause. Understand there is no ex- factor. Either you do or you don't. It can't get any simpler. I have been single since I met you over ten years ago; waiting for you to decide you were ready to settle down. You chose someone else twice. Don't invite me into your hell or try to make me feel guilty because you don't like the life you chose for yourself. I am marrying a man that I know loves me. That chose to love me." With a huge smile I explained,

"I know that Trevor would never cheat on me, I know if I got terminally ill, he would be by my side every step of the way. I know that if I died, receiving the insurance check would sadden him rather than delight him. He considers my feelings and my needs. The fact that you are here right now proves you don't love me. You want me to break the heart of someone who loves me, just in case."

"Sterling, if I agree to marry you, I may or may not hear from you tomorrow, if I tell you I won't marry you, you are going to leave here and marry another woman in a couple of hours anyway. Rather than fighting for us, you are willing to settle for something less than. You are satisfied with mediocrity and settling with someone *just cause*. I learned a long time ago, a man does not value what he does not have to work for. You have no ring, no game plan; you want to come off the bench without suiting up. Life doesn't work that way. As long as you knew I was dangling in the wind, holding on, loving you, you were ok with that. You assumed that I would wait for you and for years I did. I waited hoping and praying that you would bestow upon me your love and a commitment."

Sterling stepped towards me, with a sincere face he said,

"In real life, I love you. I admit I was scared, and I didn't know how to love you, but I am ready. You are right, being with her, I would be settling. Please don't make me settle."

"Go back to her. If I go over ground, I've already covered, I will never get ahead. I'm sorry your window of opportunity has already closed. I prayed that God would send me someone that loved me. I got that someone who loved me enough that he made me forget about you. Sterling, you were someone special in my past, but there is no future. I wish you and your girl the very best." Sterling began to cry,

"I love you; please don't hurt me like this. You know we belong together." Sterling leaned in to kiss me. I stopped him and said,

"I am dancing to a new song with a new partner. Let me ask you this, what do you love about me? How do you know that you love me? I fell in love with the man that you had the potential to be and not the person you were. Let it go, I have to finish getting dressed to marry the man of my dreams." At that moment, Trevor walked in,

"What in the hell is going on in here?"

"Honey, it's nothing. This gentleman was just leaving." Sterling dried his tears and walked towards the door. Trevor followed him.

"Say bruh, let me holla at you for a minute. You hold a special place in Sheridyn's past, but trust I got her heart. Thank you for coming here today, see you reminded her why she loves me. Life is about choices, and you chose this outcome, when you didn't choose her. I had the courage to choose love, invest in emotion, and spend time. This duet only has room for two. Listen, you hold onto those memories, because Sheridyn and I will be creating monumental moments. Excuse me, but I gotta go marry the most beautiful, perfect woman I know."

Trevor said before patting Sterling on the back and walking away. The way Trevor handled the situation further confirmed that I was definitely marrying the right man. Sterling shook his head and turned towards the doorway to my dressing room and said,

"In real life, I love you, Baby." The moment he walked away; Madison rushed in.

"Ok. So, what happened?"

"You are happy about the wrong thing. He wasn't dressed to marry me; he was dressed to stop me from marrying Trevor on his way to marrying someone else. Sterling is scheduled to get married later this afternoon. Yes, he asked me to marry him and told me that he loved me, and I told him love just ain't enough." Looking at her clipboard Naomi interjected,

"Ok, you have to walk down the aisle in four minutes and counting, damn whatever he has to say. I don't see Stedman, Stacey's or whatever his name is on my program, therefore he is irrelevant. Let's resume the schedule."

"Ok, Naomi thanks for reminding me why I hired you as my wedding coordinator." Madison got real close to me as she touched up my makeup and whispered,

"I still think this is a tragedy. Sterling is your soul mate. You and I both know it. I think you are being a hypocrite; you are marrying someone else, someone that you don't love like you love Sterling." Peace overcame me and I smiled really big.

"You are right Madison, I don't love Trevor like I love Sterling, but Sterling don't love me like Trevor does. People can only love to the capacity at which they know, understand, or experience. Love is trust, love is commitment, and love is loyalty. Love is not a scale of orgasmic screams. This is real, this is for life. I am marrying a man that made me forget about Sterling." I said.

Completing the finishing touches of adjusting my dress, I clinched my fists and smiled at myself before the full-length mirror.

"Well ladies, this is it. I'm a big girl now, I'm fixin' ta get married, I'm fixin' ta get married." I said, doing my happy dance in front of the mirror.

"Ok, now that we all know why we are here, bring your ass?" Naomi insisted as she drug me by the arm to the door where my father greeted us.

"Look at your fat face. You are so beautiful." My father said as he kissed my forehead. Looking over my father's shoulder, I saw Sterling. I smiled. Sterling nodded then walked out of the church.

I can't deny that Sterling and I had a very distinct rhythm, but there are only so many beats to a measure. Melodies are heartfelt and reach the soul, but every song has a timeless rhythm. Dance partners change as dances fade away because partners aren't promised, but the cadence of true love lasts forever.

Deondriea Cantrice

About the Author

Deondriea Cantrice is a student of the human condition, wielding the written craft to captivate the mind much like an artist wields a brush. The pages are a blank canvas on which to draw from a talent heralded by many and matched only by an imagination that rises to the task.

Deondriea developed her writing skills in high school and sharpened her literary skills by writing newsletters, short stories, program curriculum, and most notably, *When Emotions Lie*.

Now Certified Confidence and Transitional Life Coach, Deondriea provides tailored guidance, inspiring clients to shed self-doubt and embrace their true potential. Her sessions are a blend of motivational dialogue and actionable steps, designed to equip individuals with the tools needed for unwavering self-belief. She aspires to entertain, educate, and inspire her readers with tales of true life.

Deondriea greets everyone with a smile and aims to have a positive impact on everyone she encounters through effective communication, affirmative interaction and veracity. Deondriea believes, "with direction and discipline, accomplishment is attainable."

Alicia believes that her marriage with husband Arlington is a
fairytale come true - until Alicia is confronted by Piper, a
woman who claims to be her husband's girlfriend. Alicia lets
her emotions get the best of her and yields to the opinions of
her friends Cassie and Myra instead of answers from her
husband.

Will Alicia gamble her marriage for the sake of being right?
When the truth is hidden within the lie and lies tell the truth,
where do you seek the truth When Emotions Lie?
PICK UP YOUR COPY, TODAY!

@deondriea

@deondriea

@deondriea

@deondriea

@deondriea

@deondriea

www.deondriea.com